THE MASKED BALL

Justin Worthing was  the ballroom to se dance, when a v dressed him, "You around to see a w before him.

He felt rather foolish and said gruffly, "No need to stand on ceremony—or kneel. You may rise."

The lady held out her hand and he took it to help her up. He examined her curiously, for he did not remember seeing her before, and although her face was half obscured by the mask she wore, that part he could see told him that the whole was undoubtedly beautiful.

"Have we been introduced? he asked.

"Sire, I would have thought there was no need for an introduction," she said, her voice vaguely familiar. He was sure they *had* met before, although he could not remember where.

He *was* to remember later exactly where he heard that voice. But not just yet.

Also by Denice Greenlea::

THE ARDENT SUITOR   23914 $1.75

THE FORTUNE SEEKER   23301 $1.75

THE MASQUER

Denice Greenlea

FAWCETT COVENTRY ● NEW YORK

THE MASQUER

Published by Fawcett Coventry Books, a unit of CBS Publications, the Consumer Publishing Division of CBS Inc.

ISBN: 0-449-50054-3

Printed in the United States of America

First Fawcett Coventry printing: June 1980

10   9   8   7   6   5   4   3   2   1

THE MASQUER

Chapter One

Chapter One

Miss Devlin, blissfully unaware of the fate in store
for her, came down the back stairs that evening,
preoccupied with the instructions she was about to
give the cook regarding a planned picnic for her
two charges the next day. She was consulting a list
of treats the boys had requested, holding the paper
close to her face because she had left her thick-
lensed spectacles upstairs. Thus she did not see
Lord Larchmont lurking in the shadows until she
was nearly on top of him, else she might have
turned back to avoid the encounter.

"Well met, my pretty one," Lord Larchmont
said, and Miss Devlin's heart sank as he took her
arm in a strong grip and pulled her close to him.
"Do not look so surprised, my dear," he said, not
noticing the slip of paper that had dropped out of
her hand to flutter down the stairs. "Did I not hint
to you before that I might be able to offer you a

better position than that of governess? I want you to know I am always a man of my word."

Miss Devlin struggled, but was no match for his strength, and realized after a few futile moments that it would be best to submit, however unwillingly, to his embrace, for to cry out would only raise the house and bring unwelcome witnesses to the scene. Indeed, she might have got by with nothing more than a few badly aimed kisses and an even firmer resolve to avoid Lord Larchmont's company in future had not Lady Larchmont chosen that time to bid her two sons good night and, since she was just coming from her own consultation with the cook, chosen to go up the back stairs to do so. She had picked up the stray piece of paper curiously, but it was not until she turned the corner to the second floor landing that she realized where it had come from.

Lady Larchmont hesitated only for a moment, during which she considered turning back and ignoring the entire incident. She did not care overly much for scenes, and had always found it easier to turn a blind eye on her husband's philandering. But the next instant her natural indignation took over, and she drew herself up and said in her grandest and most imperious manner, "Well!"

No wife in the world could blame her for choosing to view the entire affair as the fault of the beautiful young governess and not of the noble, but sometimes weak husband. So she missed the well-aimed kick to Lord Larchmont's shin and saw only a green-eyed temptress, flushed in the heat of passion, wickedly leading her husband astray.

Lord Larchmont lost his breath when Miss Devlin finally pushed him away from her, against the wall, and what with that, the pain in his shin, and the shock of seeing his wife, he could only manage to utter a croaking, "Oh, my!"

"Well, Miss Devlin, what have you to say for yourself?" Lady Larchmont demanded, her sharp words hiding the bitter disappointment she now felt, both in her husband for bringing his indiscretions into their own home, and in Miss Devlin, whom she had genuinely liked and believed to be above such deceit.

"I am so sorry, my lady," Miss Devlin said, smoothing her unruly hair which tended to curl about her face no matter how severely she tied it back. "I assure you, I did nothing to encourage your husband. He—"

"Never mind that," Lady Larchmont cut her off. "The fact remains that I have caught you in his very arms, and you did not seem to be struggling overly much."

Though she knew it was useless to argue, Miss Devlin could not but protest at this. "That is not true! Your husband is a very powerful man, and I was fighting him with all my strength."

Lord Larchmont could have attested to this as he rubbed his shin gingerly.

"That is enough!" Lady Larchmont exclaimed, perhaps more fiercely than she had intended, for she was now trying to fight back tears and retain the upper hand. She glanced up the stairs toward where her children were sleeping, and lowered her voice. "I must ask you to leave us tomorrow, Miss Devlin, and I am sorry to say I cannot find it in my conscience to give you a reference."

"My dear—" Lord Larchmont put in, now recovered of his breath and dismayed to think that

Miss Devlin was to be sent away out of his reach, "it wasn't entirely her fault, surely—"

Lady Larchmont gave him a withering glance. "We will speak of *that* later, in private, but for now there is no reason to compound your crime by discussing it in front of your accomplice. Miss Devlin, that will be all. I expect you to leave us the first thing tomorrow morning and I have no wish to see you again."

"Yes, my lady," Miss Devlin said, her lovely eyes filling with tears. She started up the stairs and then turned back. "I am so sorry, my lady. I wish I could say something—anything—to make you change your mind." There was a catch in her voice, but she controlled her tears valiantly. "I wish with all my heart that this had not happened, because I valued your good opinion and your friendship." And she gave Lord Larchmont a final bleak look which made him conscious, as nothing his wife ever could have said, that he had perhaps acted badly.

"But of course," Christabel Devlin was saying to her stepmother the next day, "that didn't stop him from offering me a *carte blanche* before I left this morning! As if I would want to come under the care of any *man*. They make me sick, the lot of them!"

Alexis Nichols clucked sympathetically, for while she did not agree with this sentiment, she understood the circumstances that brought Christabel to say it.

"And there you have it, Alex!" Christabel declared, flopping gracefully onto one of the white settees in Alexis's elegant drawing room. "That is

10

the third position I have lost in as many months and all because of my accursed beauty. What am I to do?"

Alexis sighed and shook her head. "There is nothing else for you to do, my dear, but return to the agency and try to obtain another position."

"With no references?" Christabel snorted at this fanciful statement. "It was difficult enough the last time when I had a glowing testimonial from Mrs. Chalmers because she knew I was not to blame. But they will certainly not believe me when I claim for the third time that I did nothing to encourage the advances of husband, uncle, or brother, as the case may be." She pushed her spectacles up with one finger, then added, "And these are the only things that have kept me safe from grandfathers, sons and distant cousins as well."

Alexis hid her smile, for she knew Chistabel herself found no humor in that statement. She changed the subject, in an effort to take her stepdaughter's mind off her troubles. "We go into rehearsal for *As You Like It* next week," she began brightly, "as soon as we have finished casting. I haven't done it in ten years, but it was always one of my favorites. But do you know, that dreadful Santanos had the audacity to suggest I might be too old to play Rosalind! Thank goodness Martin set him straight on—"

"I don't suppose you have heard from any of my relations?" Christabel asked dully, having heard none of Alexis's chatter.

Alexis shook her head. "But do not be discouraged, my dear. It has only been three months

11

since I wrote to tell them of your father's death. Letters to Ireland take a very long time."

"Not *that* long," Christabel said. "If they were willing to do anything at all for me, there has been time for a dozen letters to pass between us." The sides of her perfectly formed mouth drooped slightly as Alexis gave an apologetic shrug. "What about Mother's side of the family? Has my uncle returned from the West Indies yet?"

"No, not yet," Alexis said, then brightened as she thought of something that might cheer her up. "But I have met your cousin, Lord Ingram Westham. He seems a most charming young gentleman, only a few years older than you."

This did generate a spark of interest. "I didn't know I had any cousins," Christabel said.

"Oh, yes," Alexis assured her. "In fact, you have three, for Lord Ingram also mentioned an older brother and a younger sister."

"How did you meet him?" Christabel asked with lessening interest; she did not see how having three cousins could help her in any way.

"It was during a party at the theater. Martin introduced him to me, but of course I didn't tell him who I was, I thought it better not, although he does not seem to have the aversion to actors that your grandfather held. He was quite taken with our Maisie," she laughed lightly, but Christabel again was not attending. "Chris! I thought you might be glad to hear this, for it may mean that your uncle, too, will be agreeably disposed toward you."

"Forgive me, Alex, I was thinking of something else."

"That was obvious," Alexis said good-naturedly.

12

Christabel jumped up restlessly and walked over to look at her reflection in the glass over the mantelpiece. What she saw should have given her no cause for unhappiness. Lustrous dark brown hair, dancing with gold and auburn lights, milk white skin, perfectly chiseled features, and hazel eyes which, when she removed her spectacles proved to be more green than hazel, an emerald green surrounded by a lush growth of dark lashes. But Christabel was unhappy nonetheless

"Alex, why was I not born either ugly or rich? Or at least wicked, for then I might have used my beauty to my advantage—as you did." She clapped her hand suddenly to her mouth. "Oh, dear, I didn't mean that the way it sounded."

Alexis laughed gently. "I know what you meant, my dear." Her voice still held a pleasant trace of accent, despite all the years she had lived in England. "But you must remember that I am not the granddaughter of an English peer, as you are. My father was a simple farmer, not a gentleman."

"And what good does all that breeding do me now?" Christabel asked. "It simply keeps me from doing what I most want to do in life." She knelt down beside her stepmother's chair. "Please, Alex, can't we give it up? Let me come on the stage with you! Then I would never have to be a governess again and we could forget all about my uncle the duke and all my other relations and live together very cozily. Alex, I know I would be a great success."

Alexis stroked Christabel's hair gently. "I know you would be, too, but it is no kind of life for you. You would never meet anyone suitable."

"What do I care for that?" Christabel said

13

haughtily. "I shall never meet anyone as a governess, either."

"There is always the possibility," Alexis said. "At least you will be exposed to the right sort of people."

Christabel gave an expressive grunt as she stood up. "And what has happened to me when I have been exposed to those people you call the right sort? I have been mauled in hallways and on the back stairs, afraid to leave my room after dark and making quite certain that my bedroom door is always locked." She paced restlessly. "I do not intend ever to marry—my experience with the opposite sex, I am afraid, has led me to form a very low opinion of them. I have never yet met a man who spoke to me as a person, as a fellow human being. They see me only as an object of beauty. Then why should I not use that to my advantage for once? Let me be an actress!"

Alexis shook her head. "I was there when you promised your father—"

"I promised Father a great deal too much!" Christabel interrupted. "But I did not promise him that I would lead my life as a common drudge!"

"Christabel!" Alexis admonished. "You know very well what your father wanted for you. He spent his life keeping you and your mother shielded from the theater, sending you to the best schools and making quite certain that his professional life never overlapped with his personal life so that you would not be exposed to unsavory characters."

"Like you?" Christabel asked mischievously.

"You are incorrigible," Alexis said, but with no

real anger. To those circles Stephen Devlin had wished to see his daughter accepted in, an actress was indeed an unsavory character of the worst sort, and her own history might be the scenario for many of her colleagues. She had arrived in England at the age of seventeen under the protection of a marquess, who, when it came time for them to part company, very kindly introduced her to the management of the Royal Theatre. The manager took her in hand, anglicized her unpronounceable Russian name, and carefully coached her until she had lost most of her accent. At first it was her beauty and youth alone that won her parts, but when it was discovered that she could actually act, her continued success was assured.

She had met Stephen Devlin early in her career, playing Cressida to his Troilus. He was the fifth son of an obscure Irish peer and had come to England to seek his fortune, which he found upon the stage. But while he had been on the boards for more than thirty years, and eventually managed his own theater, the Majestic, where Alexis became a member of the stock company, he had always remained a gentleman. Until his wife died there had been nothing more than deep friendship betweeen Stephen Devlin and Alexis Nichols, and no one was more astonished than she when he asked her to marry him. The marriage had been happy but too brief, and now Alexis was left with the responsibility of his lovely daughter, whom she loved dearly, but who was now proving to be nearly as headstrong as her father.

Alexis gave a little sigh and threw up her hands. "I don't know what to tell you, Christabel. I do not wish to see you unhappy and yet I cannot feel it is

15

right to go against what your father wanted for you. If there were more money, we could hire you a chaperone and introduce you to society by the front door instead of the back. But we do not have the money for that, and so you must earn your living as you are best qualified." She noticed Christabel's grimace and asked softly, "What is wrong with that? I thought you enjoyed teaching children. You were so happy when you taught at the school for a year."

"That was different," Christabel said. "I only taught because I had become too old to *be* taught, and I knew all the while that it would be over quickly, with the rest of my life still before me."

"And now circumstances are forcing you to make something of that life," Alexis said with finality.

"And it is not what I wanted," Christabel said, sinking back into the settee. "Alex, why can't I stay here and work for you? I will take care of all your business affairs and correspondence as I did for Father all last year when he was ill. You would not even have to pay me anything, I will work for my room and board."

"And a new pair of boots every spring?" Alexis asked with a laugh. "You would be bored in two days. I have so little correspondence you would find yourself with nothing to do, and constantly we will have the argument of why you cannot come on the stage." She paused for a moment's reflection. "If you cannot go back to the agency, perhaps I might be able to find a position for you. I am to attend the prince's supper party tonight

16

after the show, and while they are usually harum-scarum affairs, there are always a number of important men attending, some of whom must have children in need of instruction. I will make discreet inquiries."

Christabel laughed without real amusement. "And they will be even more certain that I will return their advances if you obtain the position for me."

"You will have to see that they do not," Alexis said equably.

"If only there were something I could do besides being a governess. I shouldn't care to be a companion to some wealthy old widow, but if I were a man, I would make someone a splendid secretary. Someone with more correspondence than you, that is."

"If you were a man, we should not have this problem at all."

"Perhaps if I disguised myself as a man—" Christabel began excitedly.

"Now you are becoming fanciful, my dear," Alexis said, rising. "No one could ever mistake you for a member of the opposite sex, however good the disguise. But now I must go and make ready for the theater. Agnes has put your things in your old room, but do not become too settled in. Tonight I will make inquiries for a position for you, as a governess," she finished firmly.

"If only you would change your mind about letting me on the stage," Christabel persisted, following her to the door. "It would not be for long—only until we hear from the duke. I can change my name and no one will be the wiser.

You said they have not finished casting *As You Like It.* I would make a wonderful Celia—'I pray thee, Rosalind, sweet my coz, be merry.' "

"Stop! Stop!" Alexis laughed, holding up her hand. "You are very convincing, but Celia has already been cast."

Christabel was not to be subdued now. "Then I could be Audrey. I do an excellent Yorkshire. I could even plump myself out and blacken one or two teeth." She stopped short as an idea suddenly came to her. "Why, Alex, that is the answer! If I were to make myself unattractive, I would be able to keep a position as a governess in the household of the ugliest lady in England!"

Alexis looked at her warily. "And how would you accomplish that?"

"Alex, really, you have a box full of paints and powders for the stage."

"But they are designed to make me more beautiful," Alexis said, smiling, "not uglier."

"Never mind that!" Christabel declared. "If you let me experiment with them, I am certain I can come up with something. Let me see, I could powder my hair to make it appear mousy, use some yellowish cream on my face for a sallow complexion, perhaps some dark shadows under my eyes, and I could wear a costume like the nurse in *Romeo and Juliet,* filled out with pillows." Her eyes sparkled behind her spectacles as she became more excited. "Alex, where are your paints?" she demanded.

"They are all at the theater, but Christabel—"

"Then I will go there with you tonight!" Christabel decided. "Oh, come, do not say no.

Father often let me wait backstage for him if I was quiet and spoke to no one. I promise I will not utter a word to a soul."

"Chris, I do not think—"

"You do want to keep me off the stage, as you promised Father, don't you?" Christabel pleaded, looking at her stepmother engagingly through her eyelashes. "Well, you never will be able to if I lose every position I obtain because I am too pretty. Besides, it will make it more fun for me, too. I can pretend I am playing a role the whole time—The Ugly Spinster. That sounds like a good name for a play, does it not? Oh, please, Alex, please."

Alexis could hold out no longer against her stepdaughter's entreaties. "Very well," she said, shaking her head at her own weakness. "I will allow you to come and play with my paints—for it is nothing more than play, my dear, and you are like a great child."

"Yes, I suppose I am," Christabel said brightly. "But you should not chide me for it—you play dress-up every night." She gave Alexis a hug. "If this does not work, I don't know what else I can do. You do understand?"

"Yes, my dear, I do."

"Of course we will have to change my name," Christabel said, becoming thoughtful again. "If I should meet any of my former employers in a new position, all would be lost. Let me see, what do you think of Miss Grimstone? That would be perfect for the character I envision."

"My dear, with a name like that I believe you would tend to overact," Alexis said. "Why don't we just call you Miss Stone? That is easy to remember and conveys the same idea."

"Very well," Christabel agreed. "Miss C. Stone, you will be born tonight."

Chapter Two

Lady Fenworth timidly knocked on the door of her brother-in-law's study, clutching in her other hand the scribbled, incomprehensible message that had brought her thither. Answered by a gruff, "Yes, what is it?", she slowly opened the door and poked her head in, not daring to go any further. She noted immediately that she had interrupted him as he was dictating to his secretary, for Rodgers sat in a chair close to his master's desk, his pen poised and ready to write again as soon as the interruption was over.

"Well, Phoebe, what brings you downstairs at this hour of the morning?" Justin Worthing asked with some surprise as he consulted his watch, for Lady Fenworth rarely emerged from her bedroom before noon and it was now but ten o'clock.

"You—you sent for me, Justin, I think," she said uncertainly.

"Did I?" He cocked an eyebrow. "I don't recall doing so." He turned to his secretary and with a brief nod of dismissal said, "Go and transcribe what I have given you thus far, and we will continue after I have spoken with Lady Fenworth." Rodgers obediently gathered up his writing materials and with a brief cough retired to a small antechamber off the library where his own desk was situated, discreetly closing the door behind him.

"Well, Phoebe, are you going to hang in the doorway all day?" he asked, trying to avoid the note of impatience that invariably entered his voice when he spoke to his sister-in-law. "Come in and state your business."

Phoebe hesitantly entered, taking the seat Rodgers had recently vacated. She avoided Worthing's gaze as best she could, glancing everywhere but at his face, for indeed the sight of that imposing visage might cause trepidation even in one of less delicate sensibilities than Lady Fenworth. Justin Worthing was not an ill-looking gentleman; on the contrary, he might have been regarded as exceedingly handsome but for a long scar on one cheek that ran from beneath his eye to his jawbone. Of course there were those who contended that the scar gave him character and mystery, although Lady Fenworth could not be counted among them and indeed would have been hard put to express an opinion on the subject one way or the other. Rather, it was the expression on that face that caused her such anguish —interruptions of any kind always caused Worthing to scowl, and the scowl reminded Lady Fenworth of a particularly harsh governess she had once had.

Cautiously, she held up the note she clutched

in her hand. "I cannot make out your writing very well, Justin, but I thought you wanted to see me at —" she consulted the paper, trying to decipher it —"at eleven o'clock, but I thought it best to come right away and see what you wanted."

Unexpectedly, Worthing threw his head back and laughed. "I suppose I should have dictated the note to Rodgers, since my handwriting is so abominable." He stood up and came around the desk, taking the note from Lady Fenworth's hand, then sitting on the edge of the desk. His informal stance helped Lady Fenworth to relax and she even smiled a little in response to his amusement.

"What the note says," Worthing explained, "is that I intend to interview a governess for Richard at eleven o'clock, and that if you wished to meet her, you should be dressed by about that time."

Lady Fenworth's smile faded at the word *governess,* coming as it did so soon after her recollection of that specter from her past. "A governess for Dickie? But why?"

"Richard is almost six years of age now, an age where he should be taken from the constant care of his nanny and put under a stricter program of study."

There was but one subject in the world upon which Lady Fenworth held anything remotely resembling an opinion, and this was the care of her son. "But Justin, he absolutely loves Nanny!" she exclaimed. "It would simply break his poor little heart to be taken from her. And he is so *delicate,* too."

Worthing sighed and shook his head. "He is not

23

delicate, but a normal, healthy boy. It is your imagination that makes him delicate."

"I did not imagine that attack of scarlet fever he had last year. Nor the time he had the mumps." Sudden tears sprang to her eyes as she recalled these distressing periods of illness. "I suppose next you will send him off to school."

"Of course he will go to school when the time comes," Worthing agreed, "but in the meanwhile he will have a governess, just as Edward and I did. Even Nanny has agreed that it is an excellent idea."

This mention of her late husband caused Lady Fenworth's tears to flow in earnest and she fumbled around for a handkerchief; finding none, she started to wipe her eyes on one of the voluminous sleeves of her jonquil yellow negligee until Worthing handed her his own handkerchief. He was well used to Phoebe's tears, for it was the way she greeted any disturbance of her usually tranquil world, and he waited patiently until she was finished.

This took several minutes, and by the time she was dry-eyed once more, Lady Fenworth had fully accepted the fact that her darling Dickie was to have a governess, and even approved of it, having fortunately remembered another governess from her past who had been kind. Indeed, if she had been asked to explain her recent tears, she would have been at a complete loss.

"I suppose it will be good for him," she said finally. "He is so clever—just like his father—and poor Nanny has trouble keeping up with him now that she is getting older."

"Just what I thought myself," Worthing agreed, returning to his place behind the desk, now anxious to end the interview. "As I told you in the note, she will be here at eleven if you wish to meet her."

"Oh, yes, of course I do," she said, suddenly delighted that she was being consulted on this important matter. "Send for me when you are ready." She arose and started for the door.

"I will do that," Worthing murmured, turning his attention back to the papers spread over his desk.

Lady Fenworth paused at the door, a puzzled expression on her face as a niggling thought in the back of her head finally took shape and formed itself into words. "But Justin," she said, "where did you find this governess? Why did you not tell me before that you planned to advertise?"

"I did not advertise," he explained, once more dragging his attention away from the work at hand. "I was introduced to someone at the prince's supper party last night who has a friend seeking such a position."

Lady Fenworth's velvet brown eyes opened wide. "Oh, Justin, you met her at the *prince's* party? Are you sure she is quite proper?" She had heard much that was shocking about the prince's late-night parties, and especially about the sort of women that attended them.

Worthing smiled slightly. "The governess herself was not present, Phoebe, only her friend. But I assure you, if she is not quite the thing, I will not hire her. Richard's welfare is as important to me as it is to you." He decided it best not to mention the fact that this "friend" was an actress—he hadn't the time for another outburst of tears.

Much relieved, Lady Fenworth returned to her bedroom to change for the expected interview.

But while he would never have said as much to his sister-in-law, Worthing too had his doubts about whether or not this Miss Stone would be quite proper. When Martin Hayworth introduced him to Alexis Nichols last night as someone seeking a post for a governess, his first thought was that they were both enjoying a joke at his expense. Even now he suspected that it might turn out to be some elaborate hoax, that Miss Stone would be another actress, painted up, and totally inappropriate for the position she pretended to desire. But he immediately shrugged the thought away; he would find out for certain soon enough, and meanwhile there was much work to be done. He called Rodgers back into the room and resumed his dictation without further delay. About an hour later, at exactly eleven, he heard the sound of the front door.

"Rodgers, that will be all for this morning. I expect this is Miss Stone now, and after I have interviewed her I will go straight to my club for luncheon."

"Very good, sir," Rodgers said, coughing slightly. He gathered his writing materials together. "I should have a clear copy of that report ready by tomorrow." He coughed again.

"Good," Worthing said, "and Rodgers, I wish you would do something about that cough. You have been at it all morning, and aside from the time I waste worrying about your health, I find it extremely irritating."

Rodgers caught the twinkle in his employer's eye and smiled. "It's nothing, sir, but I can't seem to shake it."

Worthing spoke in a gruff tone that covered his genuine concern for his secretary's health, "If you are feeling ill, take a few days off to rest in bed. I will try to get along without you."

"Oh, no, sir, there is no need for that. I feel perfectly well."

"If you say so." Worthing was vastly relieved by this assertion, for he really couldn't manage to get along without him, and Rodgers went into his own tiny chamber to make his transcriptions, coughing again.

The woman who entered after Saunders announced, "Miss Stone," should have relieved any doubts Worthing had entertained as to the true nature of her profession, but still in the back of his mind there lurked a tiny suspicion of a hoax —Miss Stone was almost *too* perfect a figure of a governess. She wore a plain, black gown, several years out of fashion, and her rather mousy hair was pulled back tightly and covered with netting. She was a bit thick around the middle and a pair of round spectacles made her eyes appear extremely small. Worthing judged her to be in her early thirties, and any member of fashion would have instantly pronounced her a "quiz."

He stood up to greet her and was immediately impressed by how graceful her movements were. One did not expect stout, dowdy persons to be graceful.

"How do you do, Mr. Worthing," she said

pleasantly, and the low, gentle timbre of her voice also struck him favorably.

"Very well, thank you," he replied, and asked her to be seated. He looked at her blankly for a moment, wondering where to begin; he had never interviewed a governess before and was suddenly struck with the notion that Lady Fenworth should be handling this duty and not he. However, he knew quite well that his sister-in-law would know even less how to go about it, so he gamely began, Miss Stone's fixed gaze beginning to unnerve him.

"I suppose you are used to taking care of children," he said, realizing at once that this was rather a stupid thing to ask of a supposedly experienced governess.

"Of course," she replied readily, betraying no surprise at the question. "I was with the Lockwoods for ten years looking after their children—two boys and a girl. However, they have now grown up and no longer need me. Before that I taught for a year at Miss Winword's School for Young Ladies." She paused after this half-truth, waiting for another question; when none came, she went on, "I understand you have only one son."

"Not my son, my nephew," Worthing corrected. "Yes, he is almost six years of age now."

"Then you will doubtless want me to begin with his letters and numbers. Does he read at all yet?"

"His nanny has taught him the alphabet, and he can write his name. Apart from that he is as yet unschooled." He paused again, noticing her hands folded neatly on her lap; he approved. "I must warn you, Miss Stone, that we would only need your services for about two or three years. Richard will be sent to school after that and there are no other children to take his place, nor are any anticipated, since my brother is deceased."

"I understand," Miss Stone said, smiling slightly.

Worthing cleared his throat. "May I ask what else you are qualified to teach him besides reading, writing and figuring?"

"Certainly," she said agreeably. "I would, of course, acquaint him with geography and history, and if he has a talent in that direction, I might teach him drawing and watercolor, although I realize those are usually feminine accomplishments. But then, all great painters must start somewhere." She smiled again. "I would also be able to teach him a little elementary Latin, if you like, although my knowledge in that area is not very vast. However, I do speak fluent French and could certainly acquaint him with that language as well."

"Very impressive," Worthing said, and subjected Miss Stone to another close scrutiny. Yes, he decided, she looked as though she would do very well. She was plain and intelligent, expressed herself well, and on whole he did not object to the idea of placing his young nephew under her care. There was only one point that puzzled him, however. "Miss Stone, would you mind if I asked you a personal question?"

"Certainly not, if it relates to my employment here," she replied.

"Not precisely, but perhaps you will be kind

enough to indulge me all the same. I am curious to know how you are connected with Alexis Nichols. You are obviously a woman of breeding, while Alexis—"

"Is not?" Miss Stone finished for him, lifting an eyebrow. "I am related to her late husband Stephen Devlin," she explained. "You may be aware that despite his profession, Mr. Devlin was very much a gentleman of good breeding, being the fifth son of an Irish lord, and I am proud of the connection, as I am proud of my friendship with Mrs. Devlin, whom you so familiarly referred to as Alexis. I hope that satisfies your curiosity."

Her tone was damping, but Worthing was well aware he had deserved the set-down. Her readiness to defend her friend raised Miss Stone several notches in his estimation, even as he realized that her relation to Stephen Devlin must be an honest one, for it appeared that she had much of the Irish in her, too. He had no doubt now that she would be more than able to deal with his rather strong-willed nephew.

He smiled slightly as he rose and invited her to follow him. "I would like to take you up to the nursery to meet Richard and Lady Fenworth, his mother."

"Does this mean I have the position?" Miss Stone asked him as she stood up, barely disguising her eagerness.

"Upon my nephew's approval, yes," Worthing said, and noted her look of satisfaction. He opened the door for her, pausing momentarily to send Saunders with a message for Lady Fenworth to join them.

They found Richard sitting upon the floor, playing with a map of Europe, while his nanny sat nearby sewing. He was a pretty child, resembling his mother in coloring, with large, dark brown eyes and fair hair. But his chin held none of the weakness of Lady Fenworth's, instead it was fully as pronounced as that of his uncle. Richard could be a very stubborn child when he wished to be.

"Uncle Justin!" he cried when he saw him and ran into his uncle's arms. Worthing promptly picked him up and swung him around by his arms as Richard giggled delightedly. Then, setting his nephew down again with the realization that such behavior must seem undignified, he said, "Richard, this is Miss Stone. Would you like to have her as your governess?"

Richard examined her unabashedly and then turned to his uncle. "What is a governess for?"

"To teach you things," Worthing explained inadequately.

"Nanny teaches me things," Richard said, sticking out his chin.

"Miss Stone would teach you even more things —she would give you proper lessons."

While Richard thought about this and continued his examination of Miss Stone, Worthing noticed Nanny sitting in the corner, watching with interest.

"I am so sorry," he said, "I have forgotten to introduce you. Miss Stone, this is Mrs. Drake, who has been with my family since my brother and I were small."

"How do you do," Miss Stone said, holding out a hand to Mrs. Drake, who shook it briskly and

31

then announced, "She seems well enough to me, Master Justin."

Worthing answered her gravely, "Your approval and Richard's were all that was wanted, Nanny."

"I doubt not his little lordship is about to make up his mind," Mrs. Drake said, and appreciated the wry smile she received from Miss Stone.

Richard had indeed been regarding Miss Stone carefully and now spoke, "Why do you wear those things on your face?" he asked, pointing to her spectacles until a discouraging look from Mrs. Drake reminded him that it was impolite to point.

Miss Stone laughed. "I wear them so I can see better."

"Can't you see without them?"

"Yes, but everything is blurry to me, just as it would be if you were to cross your eyes."

Richard promptly crossed his eyes to discover the truth of this.

"Dickie! Stop! Your eyes may freeze like that!" Lady Fenworth exclaimed as she swept into the room to find her son making alarming faces. She looked flushed and lovely, and barely old enough to be out of the nursery herself, let alone the mother of this sturdy child who continued to cross his eyes until he noticed a frown from Mrs. Drake. Worthing promptly introduced his sister-in-law to Miss Stone.

"Well, Dickie," Lady Fenworth said, kneeling down and putting her arms around him. "What do you think of your new governess?"

"I don't quite know yet," Richard replied, sounding more adult than his mother. "We have only just met."

"Richard is still making up his mind about me, your ladyship," Miss Stone said.

Richard thrust out his chin and said, "Mama, shouldn't she call me Lord Fenworth?"

Phoebe merely giggled at this as she stood up and looked apologetically at Miss Stone, but Worthing said sternly, "Miss Stone will be permitted to call you anything she likes, including a very naughty child, if the occasion demands it."

Miss Stone saw immediately that some diplomacy was required if she wished to win the approval of her charge, so she said, "I will be pleased to call you Lord Fenworth in company, but I think it would be much friendlier if you gave me permission to call you Richard in private."

Thus petitioned, the young earl was quite happy to grant the familiarity.

Lady Fenworth giggled again and then said in an aside to Miss Stone, "I think he has taken to you," and her warm, genuine smile did much to endear her to her future employee.

"Well, then, Richard, do you want to begin your lessons tomorrow?" Worthing asked him. "That is, if it is convenient to you," he added to Miss Stone, who indicated that it would be perfectly convenient.

"I suppose so," Richard said reluctantly. "Will they be awfully difficult?" He looked at Miss Stone warily.

"Not too difficult," she laughed.

"Will I be punished like the boys in the books if I don't do them?" he asked hopefully.

"You will be given bread and water for a week and not only that, but you will grow up to be

33

extremely stupid," Worthing told him sternly.

"And you will be locked in the cold, damp cellar with all the spiders," Miss Stone embellished readily. Richard was delighted.

"But Miss Stone," Lady Fenworth said, her brow wrinkling, "our cellar is not at all cold and damp, since that is where the servants live. And if there are spiders, they haven't complained of them to *me*."

"We are quite aware of that, Phoebe," Worthing said, exchanging a knowing glance with his nephew who was grinning broadly. "Well, Miss Stone," he continued, "we have established that you will begin tomorrow. If you will return with me now to the library, we can discuss the matter of salary. You have not made known your requirements, but I am certain we can come to a mutually agreeable figure."

They left Lady Fenworth in the nursery with her son, where she immediately sat down upon the floor to help him put together the map of Europe.

Chapter Three

Christabel adjusted quickly and comfortably to her new position, finding she had an apt pupil who was eager to learn once she found the knack of holding his attention. This was to allow the young Lord Fenworth to pretend that he was actually a prince in disguise who would suffer dire punishments—meted out by his wicked uncle, the usurper—if he were ever found idle or disobedient. So Richard readily sat down to lessons with Miss Stone, soon known fondly as Stoney, who also happened to be a beautiful princess in disguise. Christabel tried to discourage this last elaboration of the fantasy, since it came too close to the truth, but Richard stuck out his stubborn chin and insisted upon it, so she reluctantly agreed.

Christabel soon found a friend in Mrs. Drake, who immediately approved of her method of handling Richard, for he was, as his nanny should know, "a willful, naughty boy, but good-natured enough if brought to things in his own way." Christabel also found that Mrs. Drake was more than willing to engage in a cozy chat over a cup of tea once Richard was settled in bed, and was able to satisfy her very natural curiosity about her new employer.

"What is it that Mr. Worthing does?" she asked one evening as they were settled in the upstairs sitting room, Mrs. Drake with her sewing. "I have rarely seen a gentleman so busy."

"Aye, he likes to keep himself busy so he hasn't time to think too hard," Mrs. Drake said knowingly. "He works in the War Office, you know."

"Ah," Christabel said, enlightened.

"No, he don't like to think too hard about things, Master Justin," Mrs. Drake said again.

She was obviously waiting to be drawn out, and Christabel was not loath to do so. "What things are those, Mrs. Drake?" she asked eagerly.

"Ah, wouldn't we all like to know? But it's a great mystery it is, and I don't think there's anyone what knows the truth of it but Master Justin and that woman and her father. Even her ladyship don't know the full story."

Christabel's interest was fully aroused by now and she pressed on. "Has it something to do with that scar of his?"

"Aye, that it has. You've hit on the very thing," Mrs. Drake said, with another nod. "Master Edward came back dead and Master Justin with his face tore in half, and no one knows what become of the father."

This was truly exciting indeed, but Mrs. Drake had evidently said all she had intended to say, and would answer no more questions until Christabel asked, "When did this all happen?"

"Let me see, it must be near on six years now, for it was soon after his little lordship arrived. And Master Justin has been a changed man since, working ever so hard and never even glancing at a female. Until Lady Imogen, of course."

This was a new subject introduced and one Mrs. Drake seemed more inclined to speak on as Christabel questioned her again.

"Lady Imogen Westham," Mrs. Drake said, and did not notice Christabel start as she recognized the name of her cousin. "Master Justin has been most particular in his attentions to her. But I don't care for her myself, and Dorcas—that's her ladyship's maid—agrees with me. Lady Imogen has made herself out to be her ladyship's great friend, you see, and Dorcas don't approve. Nor do I."

"Is she very beautiful?" Christabel asked, anxious to hear more.

"Aye, that she is, but in a dark sort of way. More handsome than beautiful, I would say. But handsome is as handsome does, and if he asked me, I'd tell Master Justin not to offer for her, for she's only after what she can get, that one." And Mrs. Drake nodded briskly, as if deciding that she would tell Master Justin even if he did not ask her.

As it turned out, Christabel had the opportunity to meet her cousin Lady Imogen the very next day. She was taking Lord Fenworth for his daily walk in the park, when they would attempt to elude the spies of his uncle and escape the haunted castle, and had just opened the front door to find a lady there, about to ring the bell.

After an awkward moment the lady spoke first. "Kindly tell Lady Fenworth that Lady Imogen Westham is here to see her." She had quickly sized Christabel up and identified her as the governess, and thus suited her tone of voice and degree of civility to one in that position.

Christabel was momentarily at a loss, for she had no idea where Lady Fenworth's rooms were situated, having had as yet no occasion to wait upon her mistress there. But she was spared from any embarrassment by the arrival of Saunders, to whom she repeated Lady Imogen's name. As they waited, Christabel proceeded to examine her cousin as carefully as she herself had been examined, and found Mrs. Drake's description of her as darkly handsome to be accurate. Lady Imogen's hair was a deep, dull black, her complexion olive. In her extravagant red velvet riding habit she looked almost Spanish, an impression that was enhanced by her snapping black eyes.

With barely another glance at Christabel, Lady Imogen immediately turned to Lord Fenworth and began talking in a babyish voice, put on for his benefit. "Little Dickie, do you remember me?" Richard did not bother to answer this, since he had seen her but two weeks before and naturally remembered her. "My, aren't we a regular little *gentleman* and don't we look just like our mother?"

Christabel, who was still holding Richard's hand in hers, gave him what she hoped was a warning squeeze. She knew already that he disliked being spoken to in that manner above all

38

things, and that he was liable to make some unsuitable remark in reply. He did.

"Is she your mother, too?" he asked, looking at Lady Imogen with something close to astonishment on his face.

Lady Imogen laughed lightly. "Aren't children amusing?" she said to Christabel in her normal voice, and then, once again high-pitched, "No, she is not my mother—she is not *old* enough to be my mother."

Saunders then returned to say that Lady Fenworth was ready to receive Lady Imogen and as Christabel watched her walk up the stairs, she shook her head and exchanged a glance with Richard, rolling her eyes expressively.

"But one must make allowances for beauty," said a voice, and Christabel looked over to where Justin Worthing stood in the doorway of the library.

Christabel was nonplussed. "Good morning, Mr. Worthing," she said, embarrassed that she had been caught out in an unreserved moment. "I didn't mean—"

"No, no, don't apologize," he said, stepping into the hallway. "It is not your fault that Lady Imogen does not know how to speak to children, but fortunately she is gifted in other ways. Richard, what are you doing?"

Richard had let go of Christabel's hand and was hiding behind her, trying to wrap himself in the material of her skirt. "I'm hiding—don't tell him," he whispered fiercely to Christabel.

Christabel was trying desperately to keep her composure and balance while having her dress twisted every which way. Under Worthing's fixed gaze she felt obliged to keep her dignity. "He's just pretending."

"Don't tell him," Richard repeated, more fiercely than before.

"I'm so sorry, but I cannot tell you," Christabel finished lamely. To her surprise, Worthing's rather severe face relaxed, and he chuckled.

"Very well, then, but please, Richard, do not pull so on Miss Stone's skirts any longer. I assure you, you are well hidden." He pulled out his watch and looked at it briefly. Then, closing the case with a click, he replaced it in his pocket. "Miss Stone, I seem to have forty-seven minutes before I am due at my club for luncheon. Would there be any objections if I accompanied you on your walk?"

"Oh," Christabel said, surprised. "Not at all, if you wish to." She glanced up the stairs, wondering why he did not wish to visit with Lady Imogen.

He noticed her glance and said, "I prefer to leave them to their gossip and would do better for the fresh air. But I have one or two things to attend to first, so if you will start out, I will catch up with you in a few minutes."

Christabel agreed, and after she had disentangled Richard from her skirt, she took him firmly by the hand and they set out.

"It will spoil everything if he comes along," Richard said petulantly after they had walked a few paces. "We are supposed to be escaping him."

"Then we will have to change the game for now," Christabel replied reasonably. "Perhaps we can pretend that your uncle is a prisoner, too, and is trying to escape with us."

"Very well," Richard agreed reluctantly, "but then we have no villain."

Christabel agreed that this was a serious problem and one that could spoil any Gothick romance. "Why don't we say, then, that your uncle is under a spell which makes him wicked sometimes and kind other times?" she suggested.

"Yes," Richard agreed, delighted. "He is under a spell from the evil witch—that lady who came to call on Mama."

"Now, Richard, Lady Imogen is not a witch," Christabel admonished unconvincingly.

"Yes, she is," Richard insisted, sticking out his chin. "And you and me are under her spell, too."

"You and I," she corrected automatically.

"You and I," he repeated placidly, taking this as her acceptance of the plan.

"A fine day, is it not?" Worthing asked, taking his place beside them.

Christabel was surprised to see that he had caught up with them so quickly. "Yes, indeed," she agreed, and then could think of nothing more to say. His stern appearance made her feel tongue-tied, and she found herself wondering again about the mystery behind the scar on his face. Finally, she could bear the silence no longer and struck about for a conversational opening. "Is it very exacting, your work at the War Office?" she asked.

"Exacting?" was the terse reply.

"It is just that you always seem so preoccupied and always so pressed for time." She panted a little as she said this, for she was finding Worthing's long-legged stride a little too fast for her.

He slowed down immediately. "Forgive me, I

feel I must always be on the run, but there is really no necessity for it now, is there?"

"You did say that you had forty-seven minutes free," Christabel reminded him.

He made an automatic movement to reach for his watch and then stopped himself, saying apologetically, "Yes, and they shall be free, at least of all thought of business. But there is a bench, perhaps you would care to sit down for a while."

They had arrived at the park and Christabel was glad to sit, breathless from the unaccustomed swiftness of their walk.

"It is too bad you do not wish to speak of business," she said after a few minutes, "for I was about to ask you what it is exactly that you do."

"Mostly cover up for the inefficiency of my seniors," he answered harshly, then suddenly relaxed. "Forgive me again, Miss Stone, it is a worrisome job, as you have noticed, but there is no reason for me to snap at *you*." He paused. "What I do is arrange for the ships that carry supplies to our troops on the Peninsula. They need everything from boots and blankets to arms and ammunition, to say nothing of the money to buy their food."

"I see," Christabel said, still somewhat mystified.

"No, you don't," Worthing said pleasantly, "but I will explain if you like." Christabel nodded and he went on. "It is of prime importance to keep our armies well stocked and well fed. Wellington's strategy of extended seige demands it. My job is to see that the supplies are distributed fairly and promptly so that the men do not freeze or starve to death, and then I must work out secret routes for the ships so the French do not put all my planning to waste."

"I see," Christabel said, now meaning it. "I never considered that before—one usually only thinks of armies fighting, not eating."

"If they do not eat, they cannot fight," Worthing said gravely. "But enough of that, let us talk about you. How are you finding it with Richard?"

"He is very clever," Christabel said.

"Is he obedient, too? I know Mrs. Drake often had trouble keeping him in line at times. Do not hesitate to let me know if you feel he would benefit from a reprimand from me."

Christabel smiled slightly as she thought how nicely that offer tied in with the game she played with Richard. "There has been no need for that as yet. Richard is an active boy, but reasonably well behaved." Richard had demonstrated that activity as soon as the two adults sat down, running off to play among the trees.

"Good," Worthing said. "I feel I can depend upon you, Miss Stone. I hope you will not take offense, for what I am about to say I mean in the best possible way, but there is something about your appearance that makes one believe you are a sensible woman. You are not dressed in the latest style, but in a manner that shows good sense and decency. There is something in a plainness of countenance and dress that inspires confidence. Not that I would say you are *plain*," he started to add hastily, and then broke off as he noticed Christabel's critical eye upon him.

"You may say I am plain if you like, Mr. Worthing," Christabel said. "I have no objection to

43

that. But you also seem to be implying that if I were pretty, I would not also be sensible and decent."

"No, indeed, I did not say that," he objected.

"But I maintain that you did," she exclaimed, warming up to the subject. "You as good as said that because I am plain I inspire confidence; the corollary to that is if I were beautiful, I would not."

Worthing saw that he was being entrapped by hiw own words and attempted to extricate himself. "I did not mean anything personal by the remark, Miss Stone. I am sure *you* would inspire confidence no matter what your appearance."

She held up her hand. "Stop, Mr. Worthing, I assure you I was not fishing for compliments. And besides, I do not agree with your point. Were I beautiful, I doubt not I would inspire not confidence, but lust." She spoke from experience, and there was a bitterness behind her words.

"Miss Stone!" Worthing exclaimed, mildly shocked by her choice of language and raising his voice slightly in consequence. "A beautiful woman may excite many emotions in a man—reverence, admiration, or respect, for example—but lust is not usually chief among them."

"Indeed?" Christabel said, looking at him sharply. "But would you not agree that a plain woman is usually at a disadvantage among a group of beauties?"

"In what way? I myself would be tempted to seek out that plain woman before all the others, for her conversation is bound to be more interesting, her observations more intelligent than those of the beauties."

"Exactly!" Christabel exclaimed. "The plain woman has an *obligation* to be interesting and intelligent to make up for her lack of physical attractions, and this therefore places her at a disadvantage. The beautiful woman has no such obligation, but is free to be herself."

"But Nature is generally fair in her distribution of gifts, granting the plain woman the greater measure of intelligence," Mr. Worthing pursued.

"Not so!" she objected. "It only seems that way because the plain woman has developed what small intelligence she may have. But I assure you, there are just as many beautiful, intelligent women in the world as there are plain, stupid women."

"But surely you don't believe—" Worthing began, then stopped in embarrassment as he realized he was nearly shouting.

They sat for a few minutes in silence, watching Richard dart from behind one tree to another, obviously involved in some game of his imagination. Finally, Worthing said in subdued tones, "Perhaps you are right, Miss Stone. One can only hope then that the plain, stupid women are at least gifted with a fortune."

Christabel chuckled at this, and Worthing tried to hide a reluctant smile as he pulled out his watch and consulted it.

"I have twenty-three minutes left until I am due at my club, I'm afraid I must leave you now, Miss Stone. Richard!" he called, and the boy came running up to him.

"Are you going now?" Richard asked him.

"I am afraid I must," his uncle replied.

"May I climb the mountain first?" was the strange request.

"Very well," his uncle replied, with a brief, self-conscious glance toward Miss Stone. Then he took Richard's hands in his and the boy walked up his legs, flipping over when he reached the top.

Christabel laughed as she watched them, noticing for a few seconds a relaxed, softened look on Worthing's face that made him look nearly handsome and much younger.

"Miss Stone," he said, after Richard had climbed the mountain several times more, "I have enjoyed our little conversation and I will be looking forward to crossing swords with you again."

"Whenever you like, Mr. Worthing," Christabel said, smiling, and knew that she looked forward to this, too.

Then he bid her good day and as she watched him walk away in the direction of his club, she noticed that he took out his watch once more to consult it.

Lady Fenworth enjoyed receiving her morning callers in what she unself-consciously called her boudoir. It made her feel almost royal to sit before her dressing table, having her hair brushed and arranged by her maid, sipping tea with an amiable companion. Her late husband Edward had encouraged the practice, for he liked to see her dressed in the loose, diaphanous gowns she could hardly wear under any other circumstances, her lovely golden hair hanging down her back, rippling like a field of daffodils in the wind with each stroke the tireless Dorcas gave it.

Lady Fenworth was aware that this daily practice made a pretty scene, and it was partly for this reason and partly in memory of dear Edward that she kept it up and welcomed visitors in to enjoy it with her. However, she was unaware of the effect the scene had on her male callers, unaware that if it were not for the watchful eye of Dorcas—who always managed to find something to occupy her in the room when a gentleman came to call—her pleasant tableau might turn into a full-blown drama. She had no idea what effect her wide, innocent brown eyes had on the opposite sex, and would have simply said that most of the men she met were extraordinarily kind to her out of nothing more than altruism, had she known what the word meant or ever looked so deeply into the feelings of others.

This morning, though, her caller was a female and Dorcas was able to relax her supervision somewhat, although she did not quite approve of Lady Imogen, to whom she referred in her own mind and with Mrs. Drake as "that piece of work."

Lady Fenworth, having no such reservations, embraced her friend warmly, as though they had not made the appointment for this very meeting only the night before.

"Dorcas, do fetch us some tea, please," Lady Fenworth said, ushering her guest into a chair.

Dorcas laid down the silver brush she had been using on her mistress and with a noncommittal "Humph" went off to do as she was bid.

Lady Imogen laughed. "I don't think your Dorcas approves of me," she said.

Lady Fenworth looked at her with mild surprise. "Do you think not?"

"No, indeed," Lady Imogen replied, "but then,

I never worry what the servants think of me, their opinions are of no consequence whatever."

Lady Fenworth, who worried about the opinions of everyone because she formed so few of her own, found this statement nearly blasphemous. "But *I* certainly approve of you," she said loyally.

"Of course you do," Lady Imogen said, "but you approve of everyone, Phoebe dear."

Lady Fenworth tried to think of someone she did not approve of so Lady Imogen would not think she held her cheaply, but before she was about to come up with an example, Lady Imogen continued,

"But tell me, dear, who was that curious creature I met in the hallway with Richard? I never saw such a quiz."

"Do you mean Miss Stone?" Phoebe asked her. "She is the new governess."

"Miss Stone? I must say the name suits her— I am positive I should turn to stone myself if I had to gaze too long on that countenance. Such a sour look she gave me!"

"Richard is quite taken with her," Phoebe said, "and I rather like her myself, she does not put herself forward too much and she is most awfully clever."

"I daresay *she* does not approve of me, either," Lady Imogen said. "But never mind that—I come bearing an invitation for you. Ingram thought that if the weather continues pleasant, we might go to Richmond and have a picnic. Of course, your brother-in-law is included in the invitation, too," she added, so casually that Lady Fenworth would never guess that his presence was the most important to her.

"What a lovely idea!" Phoebe exclaimed. "I should love it above all things, although I cannot speak for Justin. He rarely takes a day off from his work."

"Then we must change that," Lady Imogen said decidedly. "For if he cannot come, I shall have to ask someone else to make up the number and what might be a congenial, family outing will turn into a dead bore."

"I will ask him," Phoebe said doubtfully, "but I do not think he will agree."

"You must *make* him agree," Lady Imogen said firmly. "For my sake, Phoebe." She gave her friend an artful glance.

Slowly her meaning dawned on Phoebe. "Imogen—do you mean—?"

Lady Imogen spoke with studied indifference. "He *did* ask me to stand up with him twice last night," she said, "and I won't say I dislike him."

Lady Fenworth was genuinely pleased at this revelation. "Imogen! We might be sisters!"

Lady Imogen laughed. "Now, Phoebe, don't start counting chickens, although there is nothing that would please me more than to call you sister. Of course, there is more than one way to accomplish that—I know you danced three times with Ingram."

Lady Fenworth blushed. "Your brother is very kind to me."

"Kind! He is besotted," but at that moment Dorcas returned with the tea tray and Lady Fenworth was spared from the further embarrassment that kind of remark always caused her.

As Phoebe poured out the tea, Lady Imogen continued in a lower voice, mindful of the listening Dorcas, who seemed to be busy mending a ruffle on her mistress's dress. "If your brother is not agreeable to a picnic, we must think of something else that he will *have* to attend. Ingram and I would love to give a ball, but with Papa away I'm afraid it is impossible."

"Justin does not like balls, either," Lady Fenworth said matter-of-factly. "When he does attend he is generally the last to arrive and the first to leave—or I'm sure he would have asked you for yet another dance last night," she added as this happy thought occurred to her.

Lady Imogen saw that Phoebe had not taken her gentle hint, so she was forced to be more blunt. "If you were to give a ball here, he would have to be present the entire time, since he would be the host."

"Yes, of course," Phoebe exclaimed, as though this were a completely novel idea. "I have not given a ball for years and years, since before Edward died. But it's such a lot of work, there is so much to be seen to it puts me into quite a flutter. Edward and I gave a ball the first year we were married—"

"Ingram and I would be happy to help you," Lady Imogen interrupted, having heard already the story of that disastrous ball.

"How kind of you!" Phoebe exclaimed, seeing no motive behind this offer other than that of a genuine desire to be helpful. "A ball would be the very thing!"

"Good, then that is settled," Lady Imogen said, finishing her tea. "But now I must run along, for I have an appointment with my dressmaker. We must meet again soon to make plans." She picked up her gloves. "Meanwhile, do at least ask Mr. Worthing about the picnic; Ingram thought a week Thursday would be a good day if the weather is fine."

"Next Thursday," Phoebe repeated, fixing the date in her mind, although the thought of approaching Justin on the subject made her tremble.

"Goodbye, then, dear." Lady Imogen kissed Phoebe on the cheek. "I expect we will be seeing you at the Altamonts' dress party tonight."

"Oh, yes," Phoebe said. "Lucy Altamont is supposed to announce her engagement to Sir Harvey tonight, so of course I will be there."

"Then I know Ingram would not miss it for the world," Lady Imogen said with a knowing look.

"Dorcas, show Lady Imogen out," Phoebe said, blushing at this renewed reference to Lord Ingram's interest in her.

"No, no, don't trouble yourself," Lady Imogen said graciously. "I am no stranger here and can easily find my own way out."

"Humph," Dorcas said once more, after Lady Imogen had made her exit. She picked up the hairbrush to complete Lady Fenworth's toilet. "I suppose that piece of work thinks she can hook Mr. Worthing?"

"Wouldn't that be lovely?" Phoebe said, finding nothing unusual in Dorcas's familiar tone.

"Maybe it is, maybe it isn't," Dorcas said cagily. "I know I wouldn't want to be married to her."

"Dorcas, you silly thing, you couldn't marry her, you are not a man," Phoebe said quite reasonably.

"I meant if I was a man," Dorcas said darkly. "I meant if I was Mr. Worthing."

But Phoebe merely giggled and thought again how lovely it would be to have Lady Imogen as a sister-in-law.

Chapter Four

Justin Worthing considered himself a patient man. He found that most things got done eventually if one held one's temper, gave encouraging, but persistent reminders, and allowed enough time for perfection to be achieved. Of course, he himself set the time limits and standards of perfection, and those who took advantage of his apparently easy nature soon discovered their mistake. For however patient he might appear to be at first, Worthing actually had quite a furious temper and woe to the unfortunate soul who felt the strength of it.

George Jenkins, unbeknownst to himself, was about to receive the full fury of that temper. For three days now he had been acting as Worthing's secretary at the request of his cousin William Rodgers, whose illness had become more serious than he first had thought. Worthing had accepted the substitution readily, expressing concern over Rodgers's health and praising his efforts to see that his employer would not suffer from his absence.

But Worthing's praise came before he had discovered that Jenkins was a lazy waster, who couldn't spell and who wrote an abominable hand. Jenkins was slow at dictation and even slower transcribing it into something that could hardly be deciphered by anyone without an intimate knowledge of his peculiar penmanship. Worthing had allowed three days for Jenkins to prove himself other than a complete simpleton, but by the fourth day felt fully justified in giving vent to his quite understandable wrath. His consultations with his watch became more and more frequent as he waited for Jenkins to emerge from his closet with the fifth—and Worthing hoped final—rendering of the monthly report.

At ten-thirty precisely Worthing decided he could wait no longer. He walked purposefully to the door of the inner office and opened it, only to find Jenkins humming a little tune as he sharpened his pen nibs, which were laid out neatly on the desk before him like a row of toy soldiers.

Jenkins looked up brightly. "Only five pages to go, sir," he said cheerfully. "Just sharpening the old pens so as to give a finer point to your words, if you know what I mean." He chuckled at his little joke.

"This is intolerable!" Worthing declared sternly.

Jenkins looked at him in some surprise—his cousin had not warned him of Worthing's temper, having never had occasion to feel it himself. "But they're ever so sharp, sir," he protested.

54

"I have no further need for your services," Worthing continued, ignoring him. "You will be so good as to collect your things and leave my house."

"But—" Jenkins began, but Worthing turned his back on him and strode back to his own desk, afraid that if he gazed too long upon that vapid face, with its mouth hanging open absurdly, he would be moved to violence. Jenkins stood up, ready to obey this last order more quickly than any others he had received from his employer, but as he had brought nothing with him, he had nothing to take away. So he carefully pushed the chair under the desk and with a final, regretful look at the beautifully sharpened nibs, he placed his hands in his pockets and ambled into the library where Worthing awaited him.

"You may take this in lieu of notice," Worthing said, handing him some money with an unmistakable air of dismissal.

Jenkins said, "Thank you," and then hesitated, as though he had something more to say.

"Well?" Worthing asked.

Jenkins smiled amiably, undaunted by this chilling tone. "I was wondering, sir, if you would be so kind as to give me a character."

"A character?" Worthing repeated with a look of mingled horror and astonishment.

"You see, this is my first position—" Jenkins started to explain.

"And one hopes it will be your last!" Worthing declared, the veins in his neck standing out. "Leave!"

Jenkins's smile finally faded. "Right, sir, thank you, sir," he said, and quickly exited.

Worthing slammed the door behind him and began striding around the room, still too angry to sit still and think rationally of what he was to do next. He felt as though his right arm had been severed, for he had the time neither to copy out the report himself nor to wait for a more qualified young man to answer any advertisement he might place. Then through the open door into the inner chamber, he noticed the pen nibs, still all lined up in formation. He walked in and with a sweeping gesture sent them all scattering and bouncing to the floor.

He felt better after this, and rang for Saunders to order his carriage out.

Lady Fenworth had not yet spoken to her brother-in-law about the proposed picnic to Richmond, nor had she dared to suggest that she was thinking of giving a ball. The right opportunity to broach either subject never seemed to arise, and Lady Imogen was beginning to lose patience with her. The picnic was already a set thing—transportation had been arranged, the menu planned, and Lady Imogen declared it wanted only Worthing's presence to make the project a complete success. Lady Imogen and her brother were also enthusiastic about helping Phoebe with plans for the ball, and had already decided between them that it was to be a masked ball, since this would give the affair some novelty, distinguishing it from the many other balls given during the course of the season.

But the time was growing short, for there were only one or two suitable nights on which it might be held and invitation cards must soon be sent out. Still Phoebe hesitated at mentioning it to her brother-in-law, until Lady Imogen exclaimed, in exasperation, "Why, I do believe you are afraid of him, you silly child!" Phoebe hotly denied this, and thus she returned from an afternoon drive in the park with her friend firm in her resolution to speak to Justin the very next time she saw him.

This was sooner than she expected, for she had been in the house only a few minutes and was still standing in the hallway leafing through the post when Worthing came in.

"Justin!" she exclaimed. "This is a pleasant surprise. What brings you home in the middle of the afternoon?"

"My report is already two days late and I haven't had any luncheon," was his discouraging reply.

For once Phoebe remained undaunted by his tone, since she was still full of the enthusiasm Lady Imogen's recent entreaties had fired in her. "Do you have a minute, Justin? There is something I would like to ask you."

He was about to bark a sharp denial at her, but caught himself in time, realizing that she had nothing to do with his present difficulties. He glanced at the clock in the hallway. "Very well," he said, "I can give you five minutes." He led her into the library and held out a chair for her, then sat down behind his desk.

Phoebe paused for a minute, wondering if she should start by mentioning the picnic or the ball. She decided upon the picnic since this was already settled upon for a week Thursday. "We are planning a picnic to Richmond, Justin, and hoped you would care to make one of the party."

"We?" Worthing asked.

"Lady Imogen, Lord Ingram, Mary Hopkins, Mr. Waters and several others," she explained. "And I thought I might bring Dickie along, since it would be a nice treat for him."

"It sounds like a dead bore," Worthing said, and was about to utter several deprecating words about the chosen company when he noticed the pleading look in Phoebe's eyes and relented. "Very well," he said, "when is this to take place?"

He was rewarded by a brilliant smile. "A week Thursday if the weather is nice," Phoebe said.

Worthing immediately consulted his diary, then shook his head. "I am afraid that is impossible, Phoebe. Unless you make it for the Sunday, I will not be able to go with you."

Her face fell. "But Sunday I am going to Lucy Altamont's for the day, and the next Sunday I must go down to Brighton to look for a house for the summer, and the next—"

"When do you have a free Sunday, Phoebe, for that is the only day of the week I can join you." He would have just as soon begged out of it altogether, but realized he had been neglecting her of late. So while he disliked picnics and did not care to eat out-of-doors, he felt it was a small sacrifice to make.

Phoebe had to think for a few minutes before she came up with a date. "The second Sunday in May, I think," she said finally. "But that is a month away!"

Worthing consulted his diary again. "Yes, it is," he confirmed, "but I will write the engagement down immediately so you may be sure of my presence."

This satisfied Phoebe, although she was a little worried about what Lady Imogen would have to say about this postponement. However, she put this out of her mind for the moment and pressed on with her next request.

"There was one other thing, Justin," she said tentatively.

"Yes?" he asked, hoping this would not involve another sacrifice, but fearing it would.

"I was wondering—" she began, "that is, we thought—*I* thought—I thought you might like to give a ball."

"You thought I might like to give a ball," Worthing repeated slowly, as though he were trying to discover some deep meaning behind this outrageous sentence.

Lady Fenworth continued quickly, lest she run out of courage before she ran out of words. "Yes, if you don't mind. You wouldn't have to *do* anything, of course, except *be* there. And share the expense—I thought we might share the expense, that is, if you are agreeable to the idea. And we would have a dinner party beforehand, of course, with all our closest friends. I suppose you would have to attend that as well. It wouldn't be until the end of May—which is weeks and weeks away. That is, if you think we should have a ball at all. I thought it would be a good idea and we haven't had one in ever so long. Not since before Edward died, and he was always so fond of dancing and balls and . . . " She faded out, having run out of possible justifications.

"Yes, of course, if that is what you want," Worthing said, rubbing the bridge of his nose with two fingers. He felt a headache coming on.

Phoebe brightened considerably at this, but still hesitated before she said, in a small voice, "We thought, that is, *I* thought it might be a masked ball."

Worthing's expression was similar to the one he had used earlier with Jenkins. "A masked ball?" he repeated incredulously.

"It would be most awfully jolly," Phoebe offered without much enthusiasm, her heart sinking as she recognized the danger signals of Worthing's approaching temper.

"Jolly? To dress up like a jackanapes in a costume that is bound to be uncomfortable, hot and generally ridiculous? Jolly? To allow the whole of London to engage in every possible indiscretion under our roof?" His expression was awful.

"I thought—" The tears came into her eyes.

"Phoebe, if you wish to go prancing about as Nell Gwynn or some dead queen, that is your business, but I'm damned if I do it!" For the second time that day the veins stood out in his neck.

"Oh, Justin," Phoebe sobbed, "there is no need to swear at me." She dabbed at her eyes with her handkerchief.

"I wasn't swearing," he said, standing up. "Devil take it! I'll show you real swearing if you want to hear swearing!"

This last was perfectly audible in the hallway where Christabel had just come in from an educational nature walk with Richard.

"Uncle's off again!" Richard cried delightedly. "Now we'll hear it!"

60

"Go upstairs to your nanny," Christabel said firmly

"But—" Richard protested.

"Go, or I'll set your uncle on *you!*"

Richard laughed and bounded up the stairs.

Just then Lady Fenworth, who apparently did *not* want to hear real swearing, came out of the room.

"Oh, Miss Stone," she said through her tears, "excuse me."

Worthing followed her to the door and stopped her before she was ready to fly up the stairs to the sanctuary of her boudoir.

"Phoebe, forgive me," he said, taking her hands in his and trying to ignore the somewhat soiled handkerchief she held. "Forgive me," he repeated, "I did not mean to lose my temper with you, but I have had an extremely discouraging day. Have your ball, if you like. I'll dress up as the biggest jackanapes of them all for you."

"Thank you, Justin," she said, a catch in her voice. She managed a precarious smile and then went upstairs to repair the damage the tears had done to her face.

"If I were not a dependent in your household, I would call you a brute," Christabel said in a quiet but clear voice.

Worthing started at the sound, having been unaware of her presence, and indeed having nearly forgotten her presence in the household at all since their one conversation of nearly a week before.

"Miss Stone," he said, identifying her to himself. "I am sorry you had to be a witness to my—er—outburst." He chose the word with care.

"Yes, I am sorry, too," she said with a slight

smile. "Sorry to see you do not reserve your punches for those who are up to your weight."

"*That* is an accusation I will not stand for," Worthing said. "I think you would find I am generally regarded as a fair and patient man."

"A patient man who is unfortunately subject to frequent bursts of temper. Do not deny it—Richard distinctly said 'Uncle's off *again!*' " She noticed the tensing of his jaw and continued quickly, "Pray do not lose your temper with *me,* sir, I must warn you that I am half Irish and likely to be the victor if it comes to a battle of wills."

Worthing relaxed and even smiled. "I stand warned." He glanced up the stairs. "Poor Phoebe," he said, almost to himself. "Perhaps it is because she is such a poor opponent that I find it so easy to take advantage of her gentle nature. I apologize again, Miss Stone, but I have had an extremely trying week. My secretary has been taken ill, as you probably know, and I have just been to see him, with promises of large sums of money and jam for tea every day, only to find that by his doctor's orders he must travel to a warmer climate."

"I am so sorry," Christabel murmured sympathetically.

"I had to sack that fool Jenkins and now I am without a secretary. Not only that, but affairs at the ministry are in a dreadful tangle, as usual. My only hope is that the duke of Duxton will be returning shortly to help clear up the mess."

"The duke of Duxton?" Christabel asked suddenly.

"Yes—do you know him?" he looked at her curiously.

"No," she said quickly, "only *of* him."

"Oh, well, he has been off in the West Indies for the past six months or some such nonsense"—he did not notice Christabel's jaw tighten—"and while he left his son to try to handle things in his absence, a more useless bounder I have never met —unless it was that fool Jenkins." He noticed that his tone was becoming strident again and stopped for a moment. "But I must not start again. Suffice it to say that I have sufficient reason to lose my temper."

"The man of reason," Christabel said, "he has rational justification for an irrational act."

"I must return to work, Miss Stone," he said, moving toward the library door. After a glance at the hall clock, it had struck him that he had just spent seven minutes making excuses to the governess, of all people, and he wished to get away before any of the other servants saw him and perhaps expected him to make excuses to *them.*

"Is there any way I can help?" Christabel offered. He looked at her with surprise. "I have quite a decent hand," she continued quickly, "I wrote all my father's correspondence when he was ill and I am quite good at taking dictation."

Worthing paused for a moment as a vision of his report to the War Office, written in a woman's decorative and flourishing handwriting, flashed through his mind—it would certainly be a novelty. "No, thank you, although it is very kind of you to offer."

"Very well," she said, "but Richard, I am sure, is taking his nap by now and does not need me for a while." Her eyes behind the thick lenses of her spectacles were suddenly shrewd. "I assure you, your letters would not be filled with unnecessary curlicues or hearts in place of dots over the *i*'s. My handwriting is much like that of my father."

Worthing paused again, wondering briefly what the handwriting of the late Mr. Stone had been like. But then he glanced at the clock and realized that he still had had nothing to eat since early that morning and the report was already three days overdue, to say nothing of all the letters that needed to be answered.

"Very well," he said finally, "I should be glad of your assistance for today at least."

Lady Fenworth's face had been restored to its full beauty and all traces of her recent tears removed when Lord Ingram Westham was announced. This came as a pleasant surprise, for her resolution to ask Worthing about the ball and her subsequent distress had driven from her mind Lady Imogen's hints that such a visit might be in the offing.

"Please show him to the drawing room," she told Saunders and then, after a final check to make sure she looked her usual self once more, she went to the drawing room to greet her guest.

"Lord Ingram," she said, holding out her hand to him, "what a nice surprise. Will you stay for tea?"

"My dear Lady Fenworth," he said taking her hand and, with an exaggerated gesture, kissing it. "To stay for tea with you would be an inestimable pleasure and one I fear I am quite unworthy of."

Lady Fenworth giggled slightly as he released her hand, and asked him to be seated. Lord Ingram was very tall and thin and, when seated, seemed to be all knees and elbows, but he carried himself well and, while rather loose-jointed, was not ungainly. He had a pleasant, humorous face, and his hair, which was much lighter than his sister's, tended to be rather unruly. On the whole, he gave the impression of being quite an amiable fellow, which indeed he was.

He was smiling at Lady Fenworth now. "But I cannot think why my visit to you should come as a surprise," he was saying, "I distinctly remember telling the fair Imogen to carry the tidings of my anticipated arrival, even so far as to mention the very moment when I might descend upon you—or is it to ascend? I have climbed many stairways to be at your side."

Phoebe giggled again. She never quite understood his pleasant chatter, but knew it was meant to be amusing and so responded accordingly. "I have good news for you, my lord," she said.

"And what might that be, my lady?" he asked, as though it were the second line in a nursery rhyme.

"Justin has agreed to hold a masked ball!" she announced proudly.

"Brave lady!" he exclaimed, jumping up and executing a magnificent leg. "You have gallantly approached the citadel, fearlessly stormed the gates and piously laid your request at the feet of the thane of the castle. Or to be more precise, you have asked your brother-in-law and he has agreed," he finished, taking his seat again.

"Yes, indeed," Phoebe said, understanding only the last part of this. "Although he was quite disagreeable about it at first."

"I doubt it not," Lord Ingram said sympathetically. "I see him almost daily at my place of employment and am often afraid to wish him good afternoon for fear of having my head snapped off. His temper is infamous."

Phoebe nodded and thought vaguely what a kind, sympathetic man Lord Ingram was, even though his hair curled in that unusual direction. "And," she continued, "he has even agreed to join us when we go to Richmond if we can put it off a few weeks. I hope Lady Imogen won't mind."

"I will bear the tidings to her myself and soothe any of her raven feathers that may become ruffled at the news," Lord Ingram promised her.

Tea was brought up and Phoebe set herself to the enjoyable task of pouring it out. It was another activity Edward had once admired her in, and she had an indistinct desire that Lord Ingram might admire her in it too. She was not disappointed.

"My lady, you make even the simple act of pouring tea a work of art, a thing of beauty, a pleasure to behold," he said, watching her with obvious admiration. That was even better than anything Edward had ever said to her, and she smiled warmly as she handed him his cup. Lord Ingram continued, "I do believe you may prove to be an inspiration to me. I feel an urgent need to write a poem about you."

"I didn't know you wrote poetry," Phoebe said, her estimation of Lord Ingram's cleverness rising even more with this revelation.

"Didn't know?" he exclaimed with mock horror. "My dear Lady Fenworth, I am renowned for it! I have even—if given the proper incentive—been known to recite my poetry before large audiences of eager listeners. And sometimes all the incentive

I need would be a tender glance from a pair of pansy eyes."

Lady Fenworth blushed, certain he meant her own eyes, although she had thought pansies were generally purple and not brown. "You do *speak* poetically," she admitted.

"My dear, you would inspire poetry from a lump of clay," he said. Then, after a few sips of tea, he continued in a more purposeful tone, "But now down to business. In my mind's eye, I see you in pearls." He looked at her critically, an artist viewing his model. "Yes, pearls on a white background, perhaps with a few touches of gold to match the sheen of your hair." He nodded, satisfied with this image. "There is no question about it, you must attend the ball as Queen Elizabeth and I will be your Lord Essex, or perhaps Sir Francis Drake—I always fancied myself something of a pirate."

Phoebe giggled again. "Shouldn't I be frightfully uncomfortable, though, with a great board in my bodice?" She blushed as she said this word and hoped he did not think her fast.

"You needn't wear one if you don't like," he said kindly, "that is what is called poetic license."

"Then I shall go to my dressmaker's tomorrow," she decided.

"Splendid!" Lord Ingram exclaimed. He finished his tea in one gulp and then stood up. "But I am afraid I must be leaving you now. Contrary to popular demand, we are fighting a war at the moment and someone needs must run it. I was only able to enjoy this interlude with you because your noble brother-in-law is playing truant this afternoon and has been unable to fix his hawklike gaze upon me."

"Oh, dear," Phoebe said, suddenly concerned. "He is *here*, in the library. I hope you do not meet him on your way out."

"If I do, it will have been worth it for the time I have spent with you." Suddenly he clapped his hand to his head. "I feel the first line of a poem coming on," he said, as if announcing the onset of a dread disease. "O gentle Phoebe, who moves with lithesome grace—" He looked at her and said in an altered tone, "I hope you do not deny me the liberty of using your name. In return I give you full permission to employ mine, not only in poetry but in normal conversation as well. One can have too much milording and miladying."

"Oh," Phoebe said, nodding shyly. She did not understand this last, but knew in a vague way that she had just given him permission to use her Christian name and had received the same from him.

"Until we meet again, gentle Phoebe," Lord Ingram said, taking her hand and kissing it.

"Of course—Ingram," she said tentatively, then reached toward the bellpull to ring for Saunders.

Lord Ingram stopped her. "No, my dear, I will see myself out—I hope to slip past the dreaded library door undetected."

Lady Fenworth giggled again as he took his leave of her.

As it happened, he was unable to exit undetected. Preoccupied with the next line of the poem he was composing in Lady Fenworth's honor, he failed to look before him and barreled directly into Christabel as he came down the stairs.

"Madam, forgive me!" he cried, helping her to pick up the sheaf of papers she had dropped.

68

"Oh, dear," was all she said as she tried to put the papers back in order as Lord Ingram handed them to her.

He treated her with his winning smile as he gave her the last piece of paper. "I hope you will not find them too terribly disarranged," he said.

"Thank you," Christabel replied distractedly, barely regarding him.

Lord Ingram was not easily put off. "I perceive this situation calls for an introduction," he said. "Lord Ingram Westham at your service." He gave an elegant bow.

Christabel, recognizing the name, looked at him for the first time. "How do you do," she said, holding out her hand. "I am acquainted with your sister. I am Miss Stone."

He took her hand briefly. "I apologize again for my clumsiness, Miss Stone. But how is it I have not met you before this? I am not an infrequent visitor to this household."

"Oh, I'm only the governess," Christabel explained.

"Only the governess!" Lord Ingram repeated in shocked tones. "Never describe yourself so! You are endowed with a sacred trust, the molding of a youthful mind, the instruction of a child who will one day take his place in the House of Lords to govern our illustrious nation!"

Christabel smiled slightly. "Thank you, your lordship, I have never considered my position in that light before. From this day forth I shall hold my head up higher and speak in condescending tones to those with less important employment."

Lord Ingram laughed, glad to meet one with whom he could converse on his own level with no chance of being misunderstood. "You do that, Miss Stone, and on your gravestone will be writ 'she did her duty for England and the Crown.'"

"Gravestone, your lordship? I shall expect a small monument at the very least—but please do not wish me in it too soon."

"Certainly not, Miss Stone."

"Is that Westham?" came a voice from the hallway; Worthing had emerged from the library.

Lord Ingram gave a barely audible groan. "Indeed it is, Worthing, and what brings you here in the middle of the afternoon?"

"I was about to ask you the same question. I see you have made Miss Stone's acquaintance," he said, nodding toward Christabel.

"And an indescribable pleasure it has been," Lord Ingram said.

"Don't waste your flowery language on me," Worthing said shortly, "just tell me if you have heard from your father."

"He is expected within the week, barring storms at sea," Lord Ingram said. "And not a moment too soon, for my pockets are sorely to let and the pater holds the purse strings."

"Good," Worthing said, then looked sharply at Lord Ingram, who had not moved from where he had collided with Christabel. "Do you plan to spend the rest of your life on my front stairs?"

"No, indeed," Lord Ingram said, grinning. "I was just taking my leave of Miss Stone." He gave her a brief nod, saying, "I hope I will have the pleasure of meeting you again," and then, with another nod toward Worthing, let himself out the door.

"Ever the gracious host," Christabel murmured.

"I haven't the time to be gracious," Worthing said shortly.

"I have already discovered that."

In spite of himself Worthing grinned. "If I did not know better, I would say you were baiting me, Miss Stone."

"I?" she asked grandly, and then laughed. "Perhaps I am, but I wouldn't be so tempted if you didn't rise to it so eagerly."

"I stand warned," Worthing said, and without further ceremony returned to the library.

Christabel shook her head after him, laughing to herself, then continued up the stairs to join Richard in the nursery.

Chapter Five

"Stoney! Wake up!"

Christabel awoke with a start and knew that she had dozed off again in the middle of Richard's lesson.

"You weren't listening," he accused her, injured.

"I am so sorry, Richard," she said, forcing herself to look at him alertly. "I cannot seem to be able to keep my eyes open. Why don't we go for our walk now? You can finish reading the story to me later." She hoped the fresh air and exercise might revive her somewhat.

"I *did* finish—you weren't listening."

"Never mind that now," she said, somewhat more sharply than she meant to. "Do as I say and fetch your coat and hat. If I sit here any longer, I will only fall asleep again."

"Somebody has been missing their bedtime."

Richard gave an excellent imitation of his nanny's voice.

Christabel laughed ruefully. "Believe me, Richard, I would happily go to bed this instant, without any tea, but I have far too much to do."

"Nanny could take me on my walk," he offered kindly, realizing that his governess must be tired indeed if she was willing to go to bed at three in the afternoon without tea!

"Nanny has been looking after you far more than she should have to," Christabel said. "Now stop dawdling and fetch your things."

But it was Christabel herself who dawdled as they walked to the park. She had indeed been missing her bedtime for the past week and was absolutely bone weary, but it was the only way she could complete the huge amount of paperwork given her by Justin Worthing. Even now another stack of letters awaited her transcription and she knew it would be another long night.

When she first made the offer to act as Worthing's secretary, she had no doubt that both of them regarded it merely as a stopgap until another young man was found to replace Rodgers. Thus she had set herself a rigid schedule, working with Worthing in the mornings and giving Richard his lessons in the afternoons, then staying up until the small hours to complete the work for Worthing, all the while confident that this would continue two or three days at the most. But perhaps she had done the work too well, for he seemed to be satisfied and had not yet interviewed any likely replacements.

Of course, she could have withdrawn her assistance at any time if she really wished to. She was still employed as governess and there had been no discussion of a raise in pay or a change in status nor did she expect one, but she found the work interesting and even exciting. To be a secretary to a government official, especially one in a ministry such as the War Office, was immeasurably more rewarding, intellectually fulfilling and ultimately important than being a governess, even to a child as bright as Richard. Nor would she have found it a difficult job were it the only one she held; all the things that made her a good governess served equally well to make her a good secretary and the training she had received under her father during his last illness proved more than adequate to qualify her for any situation that might arise.

But one week of the backbreaking schedule she had set for herself was beginning to tell on her health. In the mornings, as she applied the yellowish cream that gave her complexion its desired sallowness, she realized that she hardly needed to paint the dark circles under her eyes nor disguise the rosiness of her cheeks—the late hours she had been keeping had done this work for her. It was not wonderful, either, that she tended to nod off while listening to Richard reading from his primer—the only wonder was that she managed to keep herself awake through the morning's long dictating sessions.

But even the fresh air of the park did not revive her that afternoon; if anything, the long walk only further taxed her waning strength. She was seriously toying with the idea of turning Richard over to Mrs. Drake and going straight to bed, already forming the excuses she would give Worthing for the unfinished work in the morning.

She was not to have this luxury. As soon as she returned to the house she was told that Lady Fenworth wished to speak to her. So Christabel once again left Richard with Mrs. Drake, who clucked sympathetically over her exhausted state, and walked slowly to the drawing room to see what Lady Fenworth wanted.

She was having tea with Lady Imogen and greeted Christabel pleasantly, "Stoney, I am so glad you could spare the time to see me. Do sit down. Would you like a cup of tea?"

Christabel accepted this offer gratefully, in spite of—or more likely because of—Lady Imogen's disapproving glance at her friend, which said, as plainly as words, "You are far too familiar, my dear."

Phoebe did not notice her friend's disapproval and if she had, would probably have thought it was because she was pouring the tea incorrectly. She handed Christabel a cup and then said, with a slight giggle, "I do hope you don't mind my asking you here, Stoney. You see, Rodgers usually takes care of things like this, but since he is gone away and you are doing his work, I thought it best to talk to you about it. Really, there was no one else."

Christabel controlled the desire she often felt in Phoebe's presence to pat her reassuringly on the head and merely inquired, "What is it you wish me to take care of?"

Phoebe took a deep breath. "Lady Imogen and I have made out a preliminary list, but I think Rodgers has lists from other dinner parties we have given, so perhaps it would be best if you checked *this* list against *that* one to make sure we have not left off anyone important. Then once that list is complete, you can show it to me and I will check off who is to be invited to dinner beforehand and then give it back to you so you can make out the invitations."

"The invitations to what?" Christabel asked. The tea had done as little to clear her head as the walk through the park.

Phoebe giggled. "Didn't I tell you? The invitations to the ball. Imogen, isn't that amusing? She didn't know we were giving a ball." Lady Imogen did not smile in response.

"Now that you mention it," Christabel said, "I do remember Mr. Worthing's mentioning something about it." She smiled slightly as she recalled the exact expletive that had served as his description of the idea. "It is to be a masked ball, is it not?"

"Yes!" Phoebe exclaimed happily. "We will all dress as kings and queens. I am to be Queen Elizabeth and Lady Imogen will be Anne Boleyn, and Mr. Worthing will be—"

"Let me guess," Christabel interrupted, "Henry VIII."

"However did you guess that?" Phoebe asked, astonished.

"It was not too difficult," Christabel said dryly, giving Lady Imogen a knowing glance.

Phoebe laughed. "I *told* you she was awfully clever, didn't I, Imogen?"

Lady Imogen nodded sourly at this, just as she had done when Lady Fenworth had previously mentioned Miss Stone's cleverness.

"And of course *you* are invited, too," Phoebe added quickly to Christabel. "As Richard's governess you would probably be invited, but as Justin's secretary, you must certainly be invited." She giggled. "It's too silly—we must really send you two invitations."

"That would be appropriate," Christabel said, smiling slightly, "I often wish I were two people."

Phoebe giggled again.

Lady Imogen finally spoke. "Miss Stone, I have been longing to ask you something. Don't you feel *peculiar* acting as Mr. Worthing's secretary?"

"Peculiar?" Christabel repeated. "Do you mean as though I had eaten something nasty?"

Lady Imogen bared her perfect teeth in an attempt at a smile. "Not at all. I meant peculiar doing a job that is really meant for a man. Don't you feel it is somewhat *defeminizing?*"

Christabel smiled back with the same false sweetness. "I am secure enough in my femininity that I would not feel defeminized by an occupation." Lady Imogen raised an eyebrow, as if she herself had doubts regarding Miss Stone's femininity. "But of course this is only temporary, until Mr. Worthing finds someone who can permanently replace Rodgers."

"Of course," Lady Imogen agreed, "one could not really expect a woman to fill the position as successfully as a man."

Christabel felt her temper rising, irritated by Lady Imogen's implication that she could not perform the job as well as anyone—male or female. "Unfortunately, Lady Imogen, it is backward thinking such as that that makes the lot of those of us who must earn our own living so difficult."

Lady Imogen's lips tightened. She was annoyed not so much by Christabel's words, which she took for so much nonsense, but by the fact that she had addressed her as "Lady Imogen," and not "your ladyship," as better suited her inferior social position.

Christabel set down her cup and rose. "I believe I know where Rodgers kept the list you spoke of, my lady. I will check it as you suggested. Thank you for the tea."

"You are welcome, I am sure, Stoney," Phoebe said, without any decrease in her natural cheerfulness, for she had understood little of the conversation immediately preceding. "You are so kind."

"Your ladyship," Christabel said, giving her a slight curtsy. Then she nodded curtly to her cousin, saying, "Lady Imogen." She could barely suppress the bubble of laughter that threatened to pop at Lady Imogen's reaction to this deliberate insult, and was sure she heard Lady Imogen say, "Insufferable!", as Christabel closed the door behind her.

She walked slowly up to the nursery, determined to leave the list and everything else until morning and take her much-needed nap. But as she came through the door, ready to tell Mrs. Drake of her plans, she was surprised to find Worthing there, too.

"There you are, Stone!" he exclaimed. "I have been searching all over for you."

"I was with Lady Fenworth," she explained.

He barely listened to this explanation, but continued excitedly, "The duke of Duxton has finally returned today, none the worse for his sea journey, I am happy to report, and eager to return to his duties. I would like to prepare a progress report for him, to inform him of what has occurred during his absence. Nothing too long, of course, say about twenty or thirty pages. A general outline, you might call it. Do you think Richard can spare you for the rest of the afternoon?" He glanced at Mrs. Drake, who was busy over her sewing.

Christabel sank wearily into a chair. She had thought herself too tired to lose her temper, but supposed her recent bout with her cousin must have revived her. In a terribly calm voice, which should have been a warning to Worthing, she said, "I am afraid that would be impossible."

"Impossible? What do you mean?"

Mrs. Drake looked up with a sudden spark of interest and the barest hint of a smile. Richard, too, was watching the exchange eagerly.

Christabel stood up, took a deep breath and looked at Worthing steadily. "Mr. Worthing, for the past week I have been performing both the duties of a governess and of a secretary. Anyone else might have thought either position enough to occupy all the energies and talents of a single person, but I have done both—competently and efficiently, I might add. Every night I have sat up until three in the morning, writing your interminable and generally boring letters and reports"—this was untrue, she usually found them all very interesting, but she was rolling now and could not stop—"I have not complained when I have gone for days with only three or four hours of sleep each night. I have not complained when, daily expecting you to find yourself a permanent secretary, I have once again been called into your library to take dictation from you, to compose readable letters and reports from your lengthy and repetitive ramblings." This also was untrue, Worthing had a succinct and pointed literary style. "I have not complained when each afternoon I had to sit down with Richard to give him his lessons, take him on outings, try to teach him all that is necessary for a future peer to know"—here she borrowed freely from Lord Ingram—"all the while knowing that once again I would receive only three hours of sleep that night."

She was pacing back and forth, making each point with a sweep of her arm, playing off her audience and gathering confidence from their rapt attention. If she had been calm enough to look at herself objectively, she would have been reminded of her father performing one of Hamlet's soliloquies, or more probably one of MacBeth's.

"But, Mr. Worthing," she continued, "the time has come for us to make a choice, a decision. I cannot go on like this, I am at the point of collapse. You must decide whether I am to continue as Richard's governess or as your secretary. I can no longer do both!" She finished finally and sat down again, worn out by her histrionics.

Worthing was strangely quiet, completely subdued by this lengthy speech. "I am so sorry, Miss Stone," he said finally, "I had no idea you had been losing sleep. I fear I have taken your efficiency too much for granted."

"Yes, indeed," Christabel agreed decidedly.

"You are right, of course," he said. "One person cannot do the work of two. I should have known better than to accept your offer of assistance in the first place, it is not woman's work. Tomorrow I will begin in earnest to find a new secretary. I certainly don't want Richard to suffer from my selfishness."

"Thank you," Christabel said, but her triumph was hollow. In spite of the fact that she knew he spoke the truth—that it was not women's work—she had still hoped he would prefer her in the capacity of secretary. But such a decision would doubtless be so unconventional that it might leave him open to ridicule, and from his point of view he had made the only possible choice.

"I can only thank you for all the help you have given me this week," and with that Worthing turned to leave. Christabel saw Mrs. Drake looking at her sympathetically and shaking her head, and she gave a defeated little shrug of her shoulders.

"No, by God!" Worthing suddenly exclaimed, turning back into the room.

Christabel looked up at him questioningly.

"Governesses are as plentiful as beans, but you don't often find a good secretary, one who understands you, who knows what you are going to say before you say it. Miss Stone, I would like to keep you on as my secretary. Naturally, there will be a corresponding increase in your salary, and one of your first duties will be to find another governess for Richard." He paused and cocked an eyebrow inquiringly, "That is, of course, if you are agreeable to such an arrangement."

"Perfectly," Christabel said, trying hard to keep a note of triumph out of her voice.

"Splendid," he said, satisfied. He pulled out his watch and consulted it. "In view of your exhausted state, you may have the rest of the day off, but we will begin that report I mentioned promptly at eight tomorrow morning."

After he left, Christabel could barely restrain a whoop of joy. "Well, Mrs. Drake, what do you think of that?"

"I think you may be good for Master Justin, since he needs someone who can stand up to him. But I think Master Richard will be sorry to lose you."

Master Richard, who had enjoyed the preceding scene immensely, just that moment realized what it would mean to him and began to cry lustily. Christabel and Mrs. Drake had all they could do to calm him down and it wasn't until Christabel promised him faithfully that she would continue her practice of telling him bedtime stories that he finally settled down and accepted Stoney's new status.

"A most irritating man," Christabel told Alexis. "Annoying, insensitive, the tiniest bit pompous and always looking at his watch as if he had somewhere important to go." She smiled, "I like him."

Alexis looked at her indulgently. "Yes, I can tell. In fact, if you say any more terrible things about him, I would swear you are in love with him."

"In love?" Christabel repeated, horrified. "Certainly not. I think that is one of the chief reasons I like him so well—for neither of us has the least chance of falling in love with the other. Mind you, I have little doubt that if he saw me as I really am he would declare himself to be in love with me and make as great a fool of himself as any man."

Alexis smiled wryly. "Vanity, my dear, is a sad failing in any woman, however beautiful she may be."

"Fortunately, it is a fault our Miss Stone cannot fall prey to," Christabel said, grinning. They were seated in Alexis's elegant white drawing room, Christabel lounging back on the sofa, the stuffing she had removed from her waist almost immediately upon her arrival making an untidy heap on the floor.

"I believe," she continued thoughtfully, "that we get on well because our tempers are the same length. Next to sharing a sense of humor with someone, I think that is most important. After all, one does feel so foolish getting angry all by oneself. It is much more comfortable when you have someone to get angry with—or *at.*"

"Yes," Alexis agreed, "I found the same attraction with your father."

"But I did not come here to discuss Mr. Worthing," Christabel said, sitting up straight. "I came to see if you have any news. I know that my uncle the duke has returned, for we have spent the last three days preparing a report for him. Has he answered your letter yet?"

Alexis shifted uncomfortably—she had been avoiding this very topic successfully until now. "Yes, I received a letter from him yesterday," she said slowly.

"It is bad news, I can tell by your face." Christabel slumped back in her seat.

"Well, it is not good news," Alexis admitted. "Here, I will read you what he says." She walked over to the writing desk and pulled out a letter. "He begins with the usual formalities. He thanks

83

me for my letter, hopes I am well, is sorry to hear of your father's death, for the stage has lost a great performer. He makes rather much of that, I think," she added, with a glance at Christabel.

"Go on," Christabel said, her lips tight.

Alexis read on: " 'I regret that I find myself unable to do anything for my sister's daughter—' "

"He cannot even bring himself to call me his niece!" Christabel exclaimed.

" '—but when I severed all connection with my sister it was final. If, however, my sister's daughter finds herself in desperate straits, I would consider allowing her an annual income of fifty pounds, but since you did not mention such a situation in your letter, I assume that this is unnecessary and that Miss Devlin is capable of earning her own living.' "

"I expect he thinks I am doing something totally disgraceful."

"Hush, Christabel, I am sure he does not." Alexis continued: " 'As to the estates in the West Indies, which were to be my sister's upon her marriage, when she did not lay claim to them, all title reversed to me, and any court of law would support me in my claim, for I have invested sums of money and have seen to their general well-being and maintenance over the years. Indeed, I have just returned from a lengthy visit there. And so, Mrs. Devlin, while I appreciate your eloquent letter, I am afraid I cannot find it in my heart to acknowledge my sister's daughter beyond what I have already mentioned. Yours, etc.' " Alexis folded the letter and replaced it in the desk.

"He offers me fifty pounds a year and considers his duty done!" Christabel exclaimed, jumping up. "The unmitigated gall of the man! He deserves his wretched daughter!" She looked at Alexis questioningly, "Do you think he is right about the legal aspects? The land was left specifically to my mother in my grandmother's will."

"I do not know for certain, Chris, but I do think it would be difficult to win a suit. After all, he is the duke and you are—"

"The black sheep. It is simply too bad. *Damn!*"

"Christabel!" Alexis admonished.

"Forgive me, Alex, it is a habit I picked up from my employer." Christabel was silent for a few moments before she burst out again. "I don't really mind so much about the estates, for I am sure he is right that I have no claim to them. What I do mind is that someone like my cousin Imogen has the right to talk down to me—that everyone who matters has the right to talk down to me because I am nothing more than a lowly governess. If the duke would simply acknowledge me, recognize my claim, my *right* to take my place among all the Lady Imogens, it would be enough."

"Christabel, that is a childish attitude."

"Perhaps it is, I don't care. But don't you see that as I am now, I belong wholly neither to one world nor the other. I am worse than an orphan, for while I have no family that recognizes me, I cannot enter fully into your world of the stage because of that same family. It is unimaginably frustrating."

"I do understand, Christabel, and I know it is awkward for you, but you are not the only young lady in such circumstances. There are many who have learned to make their way as governesses."

"And is that all my life is to be? An endless succession of naughty, untaught children until I am too old or feeble to work any longer? And then what?"

"You are painting an unnecessarily black picture for yourself, darling," Alexis said with a gentle smile. "Who knows when you will meet some nice gentleman who will wish to marry you."

"I don't want to be married!" Christabel cried. "I want to be famous and admired, and to do something creative with my life. I want to be an actress."

Alexis sighed. "You know that is impossible, and that your uncle's acknowledgment would hardly help you there. My suggestion would be to accept the fifty pounds a year he offers. With that and your new position as Worthing's secretary, you could live quite comfortably. Many young ladies are happy with less."

"What?" Christabel exclaimed. "Let him think he can buy me off and then forget about my existence?"

"It is more than I expected of him," Alexis admitted.

"And so I am to be doomed forever to a life of servitude," Christabel said glumly.

"Oh, very well, Chris," Alexis said with unaccustomed sharpness. "If it will make you any happier, I will call upon him and try to convince him how important it is to you. Although I don't see it myself."

"Alex, you're an angel," Christabel cried, throwing her arms around her. "And I'm a selfish beast." Then, with a wicked twinkle in her eye, "And if he still says no, have I your permission to see your producer—Santanos, is it?—about a position in the Majestic Theatre?"

Alexis laughed. "You are incorrigible. Yes, you have my permission, for all the good it will do you. Santanos is not particularly interested in running a professional theater, but cares more about catering to the gentry—holding masquerades or amateur theatricals every Monday night. If he hired you to appear in a show, I would be very surprised indeed."

"Then I will go to Martin," Christabel said, "he was always an admirer of Father's and he once told me I would make a glorious Juliet." Then, glancing at the clock on the mantel, she hastily began replacing her stuffing. "Oh, dear, I really must go now, I didn't know it was so late. It was difficult enough finding two hours in a row to come and see you." She suddenly laughed. "I'm picking up all kinds of bad habits from Mr. Worthing—now I am forever looking at the time. I will have to buy a watch of my own soon."

"I will do my best with the duke," Alexis promised, then with a knowing smile, "but meanwhile I am sure you will be enjoying your new life."

Chapter Six

Lady Fenworth barely noticed the change in Miss Stone's status, but had she been able to express an opinion, it would be that she preferred the new arrangement. While she had been content to see her offspring under Miss Stone's capable hands, Phoebe found her of much more personal use as Justin Worthing's secretary, especially in helping to plan for the ball. And Phoebe *liked* Miss Stone. She never felt stupid or silly around her, as she did with dear Lady Imogen, who always seemed to lose her patience when Phoebe missed the point of an amusing anecdote or was late for an appointment. No, Miss Stone was a great *comfort* to Lady Fenworth, and she could not remember how she had ever got along without her.

As for Justin Worthing, he too was more than satisfied with the arrangement. Miss Stone was fully as competent as Rodgers had been and more personable, so that he found himself enjoying her company as well as admiring her efficiency. She even had a head for figures and an excellent memory, both valuable assets when writing out the long, tedious requisition lists for supplies. Stone could remember almost to the exact amount what they had put on which ship and what was left in the warehouses, saving them both a great deal of time.

After about two weeks Worthing had become so used to his new secretary that he thought nothing of asking her to accompany him to the War Office one afternoon to check on some figures. He was surprised by the stares his entrance into those sacrosanct premises with a female elicited, and cautiously felt the seat of his pants to see if that might be the cause of his colleagues' gasps and titters as they stuck their heads out of their respective doors to watch him pass. The true reason for this reaction did not cross his mind until a few minutes later when the duke of Duxton walked in on him after a peremptory knock.

"See here, Worthing," he said in a fine fluster, "what is the meaning of this?"

Christabel looked at him with interest, for this was the first time she had laid eyes upon her uncle. She knew that Worthing admired his judgment and considered him a capable administrator, but her own experience of him through the letter he had written to her stepmother and various remarks made by Lord Ingram made her think of him as a hard man, quite tight in the pocketbook, and she had pictured him tall and thin, with a hard-set jaw, a cruel twist to his smile and his daughter's narrow black eyes. Thus, she was surprised to see that he was none of these and did not fit her mental image of him in any way. Instead, he was short and thickset, but not unhandsome, and his eyes were not so much like those of Lady Imogen, but more like those of Christabel's mother—the sister he had refused to acknowledge. She found the resemblance disconcerting.

Worthing had been in the middle of reading through some dispatches that had just arrived and, thus interrupted by the duke, had no idea what he was referring to and said so.

"I mean bringing a woman here, Worthing!" Duxton exclaimed in a heated voice, trying to ignore Christabel's presence. "Bringing a woman into government offices!" Then raising his booming voice even louder, "Have you lost all sense of propriety and decency? This is not a tearoom, it is the heart of the greatest nation on earth. His Majesty would not stand for it!"

Worthing gave a wry smile. "I admire your patriotism, Duxton," he replied calmly, "but it seems to me that His Majesty is rarely in a frame of mind to stand for anything." He glanced at Christabel, who was hiding a smile. "However, permit me to introduce my secretary, Stone."

"Your secretary!" the duke exclaimed, astonished.

"My new secretary," Worthing amended. "You may recall Rodgers, my former secretary. An unexceptionable young man who will certainly go far, but unfortunately he was taken ill and has since set sail for a warmer climate. Stone more than adequately fills his shoes."

"This is highly irregular, Worthing," the duke

said, calming down somewhat. "I don't know what will happen if Liverpool should get wind of it."

"Is there a new rule that we must not allow our secretaries to accompany us here?" Worthing asked earnestly.

"Of course not, don't be frivolous, Worthing. But you know damn well that no one has ever had a female secretary, it is completely unheard of." He gave a quick glance to Christabel, whom he had been studiously ignoring until now, to see if perhaps he should have said, "lady," but decided "female" was good enough.

"The truth is, Duxton, the issue of my secretary's gender never occurred to me. I am far too busy to waste my time worrying about trivial details such as that."

The duke decided to take offense at this, for it implied that he was not too busy to do so. Besides, it had been a slow day until now, his son had been particularly vexing that morning and his daughter too had requested a larger allowance even after he had refused the same for his son. He was itching for a fight. Worthing always gave him a good run for his money, and there were never any ill feelings afterward.

"Worthing, I trust you will be able to maintain this careless attitude when you and your *secretary* have become the laughingstock of the ministry." He spoke slowly, carefully, enjoying every syllable.

Worthing eagerly rose to the bait, for he too was ready to lose his temper by now. "I hardly think anyone will waste his time laughing at *me* when there are other, more prominent candidates for that position, Duxton," he said. "For instance, those who are constantly forced to cover up for the incompetency of their relations."

Duxton advanced upon him. "Are you implying that my son is incompetent?" he demanded.

"Did I say son? No, I said relations, but if you feel that to be a personal slight, then so be it."

"I would much rather stand up for my son, Lord Ingram Westham, heir to all my unentailed wealth, and destined for a great future in politics, than try to pass off my fancy-woman as my secretary." Another glance at Christabel, who was calmly regarding him from behind her spectacles, her mousy hair in its usual severe style showed him how ridiculous this accusation was, but he let it stand.

Worthing jumped to his feet. "Now you have lowered yourself to base insults! Duxton, I had thought better of you."

"Sir, yours was the first insult when you disparaged my son—the flesh of my flesh, the blood of my bl—"

He was waxing poetical now and Christabel saw that it was time for her to speak. "Gentlemen, please," she said firmly, "I realize you are both enjoying yourselves, but I feel compelled to stop you before you resort to fisticuffs. Mr. Worthing, I am quite prepared to defend my own honor and integrity if the need arises. Your Grace, may I suggest you leave us to the business of running this office, which pursuit we were both engaged in before we were interrupted."

The duke finally looked at her directly. "Miss—er—"

"Stone," she supplied graciously.

"Miss Stone, surely you must feel yourself to be

out of place here? Why do you not take the advice of a man of experience and go home to your embroidery." He spoke condescendingly.

Christabel smiled faintly. "I am afraid that would be impossible, Your Grace. I do not embroider."

"That makes no difference," the duke said, dismissing this utterly fantastic statement. "There are a great number of other things you can do that would be far more suitable than this."

"Until I met you, Your Grace, with your vast experience, I had thought *this* perfectly suitable for my talents and my position in life. But please, advise me! Tell me what *would* be suitable." She spoke earnestly, as if she really desired to know.

"Stone," Worthing said warningly, for by now he recognized the gleam in her eyes, though it was clouded by the thick lenses of her spectacles.

Christabel continued: "Perhaps you see me as a companion to some elderly female suffering from a permanent attack of vapors. Or there are other occupations for females that you may not think quite as *suitable* but perhaps more appropriate. For instance, I might become a *fancy-woman*."

"Miss Stone!" the duke exclaimed.

"I am so sorry, Your Grace, I did not mean to shock you, but it was from you I learned the phrase." She smiled sweetly.

The duke suddenly chuckled, for the vision of this paragon, with her thick waist and sallow complexion, as anyone's light-o'-love was too ridiculous to be entertained. "Very well, Miss Stone," he said, "I see you are quite capable of defending your position. But, Worthing, I am still of the opinion that you would do better with a man. Miss Stone may perform her duties adequately, but you must consider that she is actually stealing a job from some bright young man of good family who would use the position as a stepping-stone to more important things."

"And once more leave me without a secretary," Worthing said wryly. "I am sorry, Duxton, that argument holds no weight with me. I intend to keep Miss Stone on."

"Perhaps his grace would prefer to see you hire someone such as Jenkins?" Christabel offered. "He certainly seemed a bright young man."

"Jenkins," Worthing groaned.

"Who is Jenkins?" the duke asked.

"A singularly inept fool whom I had in my employ for three days and who made a botch of everything," he explained. "No, Duxton, I will keep Miss Stone, as I said, and you may tell that to Liverpool, too, when you see him." He pulled out his watch and glanced at it.

The duke knew Worthing's stubbornness well and while he might have enjoyed arguing the point a bit longer, also knew that it would be useless. He turned to Miss Stone and gave her a brief farewell bow, thus acknowledging that she had won the field for the day. He was about to return to his own chamber when Worthing stopped him, saying,

"Duxton, have you seen this?" He held up one of the dispatches that had been on his desk.

"What is it?" the duke asked.

"One of our supply ships has been taken!"

"What?" the duke exclaimed, snatching the paper from Worthing and reading through it quickly. "The *Prosperity*. But this is impossible, the routes of these ships are clothed in secrecy, as you well know."

"Only one thing comes to mind," Worthing said gravely, "and that is that the French are somehow in on our secrets."

Duxton looked at him in perplexity for a moment. "Do you mean a spy? No, I cannot believe that. This information goes no further than this office. It was nothing more than pure luck on the part of the French. After all, we have lost ships before."

"Of course," Worthing said, but did not seem convinced.

"Very well," the duke said, "if it will put your mind at ease, I will tell my son to look into it. That is, if you think him capable," he added with a note of sarcasm, for Worthing's earlier remark about Lord Ingram still rankled.

"I think that would be a very good idea," Worthing said.

"Then I will put him on it right away," the duke said decisively, then with another short bow to Miss Stone he abruptly left.

Christabel worked the rest of the day with indifferent attention, still startled by her first meeting with her uncle. While he had not conformed in any way to her villainous image of him, she still could not find it in her to like him. She could not forget the insult he had offered in the form of fifty pounds a year, nor could she forget his still-firm resolution not to recognize her as a member of the family, more than twenty years after the original breach.

However, she was prepared to revise her opinion of him should she learn that her stepmother had favorable news on his behalf after her visit to him, but she was unable to see Alexis until the following Tuesday. The loss of the *Prosperity* necessitated a great deal of juggling of supplies on each of the ships to be sent out during the next few weeks, and thus there was more work than ever. When she finally did manage to get away, she went to visit Alexis at the Majestic Theatre, a situation that was bound to win disapproval.

Alexis Nichols noticed her stepdaughter's reflection in her dressing table mirror and turned around quickly. "Christabel! Have I not told you that you must never visit me here at the theater? It is not the place for a young lady. You are very naughty!"

Christabel laughed as she gave Alexis an affectionate hug. "I hardly look like a *young* lady when I am dressed as the respectable Miss Stone. I doubt anyone will look at me twice. Besides, this was the only time I could get away and I simply had to see you."

"I still say you are naughty," Alexis said and turned to the glass once more to finish applying her stage makeup. "But it is good to see you. Would you care for some sherry? I have a bottle in the cupboard here."

"No, thank you."

"Then sit down and tell me what has brought you here."

Christabel took a seat and faced Alexis's reflection. "Whom do you think I have finally met?" she asked importantly, but without waiting for a reply she answered her own question. "The duke of Duxton!"

Alexis gave a little "ah."

Christabel continued, "Of course, I knew I was

bound to meet him one day, for he is in the same ministry as Mr. Worthing. If I did not know anything about him, I think I *might* have found him quite tolerable," she admitted, "but he has a foul temper and antediluvian ideas about a woman's place."

"I found his temper quite ordinary," Alexis said quietly.

"Then you *have* seen him!" Christabel exclaimed. "What did he say? Do you think he will come around? Did he even receive you?"

"Oh, yes, he received me. He was most gracious—he offered me a sherry and told me I was one of his favorite actresses."

"But what did he say about *me?*" Christabel demanded.

Alexis avoided her reflected eyes. "Once again, he refused," she said. "He repeated the offer he had made in his letter, but said that his conscience would allow him to do no more."

"His conscience! I should think that would tell him he has not done enough!"

"I said something like that to him," Alexis said, "but he explained to me that your mother's action in running off with your father broke his father's heart and ultimately led to his death."

"*That* is utter nonsense," Christabel said firmly. "You know very well that my grandfather always had a weak heart, as did my mother. Did you tell him that?"

"No, I did not," she admitted.

"Why not? You should have made him feel that he is shirking his familial obligations. You should have made him feel guilty—*I* would have."

Alexis smiled slightly. "It is my opinion that one

does not show one's temper to a man of that nature. It is much more effective to be pleasant, gracious and feminine. But then, we each have our own methods. For instance, I have no doubt you had a rousing row with his grace when you met him."

"Yes, I did, as a matter of fact," Christabel said with a rueful grin. "Of course, he began it with Mr. Worthing, but I felt obliged to do my bit."

"So," Alexis said with a nod. "For me, I felt that the subtle approach would be best. I felt that if I remained on good terms with the duke, it would do more to advance your cause."

"You should be in the Foreign Office—you would make a splendid diplomat," Christabel said. "And did your approach work?"

"I think so," Alexis said, finishing her makeup and turning around to look directly at Christabel. "Do not be angry with me, darling, but I am to have supper with him after the show tonight."

"Supper with him!" Christabel exclaimed. "Alexis, you don't plan to have an *affair* with him, do you? I hardly see how that would present me in a better light."

"Christabel! How can you speak to me like that?" If it had been in her nature to pout, she would have done so.

"I am sorry, Alex," she said, immediately contrite. "I know you better than that."

"I should certainly hope so," Alexis said with a little sniff. "I am seeing the duke entirely on your account. I accepted his invitation only as an opportunity to talk casually with him, so that in such casual talk I might be able to bring you into the conversation."

Christabel hugged her impulsively. "You are a dear, Alex."

A knock came on the door and a young man stuck his head in. "Fifteen minutes, Missus Devlin."

"Freddie!" Christabel exclaimed, recognizing him. "Do you remember me?"

Freddie regarded her blankly for a moment, then clapped his hand to his head when he realized who she was. "If it ain't Miss Devlin! I didn't know you in that getup. What's it for? Don't tell me you've taken up acting—your father wouldn't approve, Miss." He regarded her suspiciously.

"No, Freddie," Christabel laughed. "Although I would like to. These are merely my respectable clothes to suit my respectable position. And how are you?"

"It's not the same here since your father kicked off, make no mistake, miss," Freddie said, rolling his eyes. "That Spanish cull don't take no interest at all in goings-on here, but Missus Devlin could tell you better about it than I could, miss."

Christabel looked at Alexis questioningly.

"I prefer not to think of it myself," she said, reaching to ring for her maid. "On the opening night of a new show it is unthinkable that the manager should not be present."

"Opening night!" Christabel exclaimed. "I didn't know or I should have brought you flowers."

"That is not important." The maid, Agnes, came in with her costume and Freddie discreetly withdrew. Alexis continued as Agnes helped her to dress. "This man cares for nothing but the money the theater can bring in—the quality of the performance does not concern him in the least. He is what your father used to call a cit."

99

Christabel clucked sympathetically. "Perhaps he was called away on important business."

"Nonsense!" Alexis declared. "He was here last night for his wretched amateur theatricals, where he allows all the noblemen in England to play havoc with our stage and scenery."

"Can Martin do nothing about him?" Christabel asked. "As the director, surely he should have some influence."

"Bah! Martin is too busy acting as producer, stage manager, and leading actor to have any time to take Santanos in hand."

Agnes nodded at this. "Fair running himself ragged, Mr. Hayworth is."

"But enough about him!" Alexis said impatiently. "I do not mean to chase you away, Christabel, my dear, but I need a few minutes alone to collect my thoughts before I perform."

"Of course," Christabel said readily, standing to leave. "Would you mind, though, if I looked through the costume room? I wish to borrow a costume."

"Borrow a costume? Whatever for?"

Christabel smiled. "Mr. Worthing is giving a costume ball, and I wanted something special to wear for it."

"Yes, of course," Alexis said absently, already assuming her character for the play. She pointed to a door at the far end of the room. "Everything is kept in there, as you know. Take what you like, Agnes will help you with any alterations if you need them."

"Thank you, Alex, and good luck tonight," Christabel said, meaning more than just the performance.

Chapter Seven

After her initial, precedent-breaking visit there, Christabel soon became a familiar figure in the chambers of the War Office and her presence was casually explained to the uninformed as "Oh, that's just Worthing's secretary, Stone. Frightfully good chap." Eventually, even those who had most strongly objected to the female invasion grew to accept her, and it was rumored that Lord Liverpool himself was thinking of hiring a female secretary.

"Although I doubt even *that* would help the Tories in the next general election," Worthing confided to her.

They had laughed together over this and Worthing once again appreciated the sense of humor and the sense of order Stone had brought to his professional life. This well-being also extended into his personal life, but here under the figure of

Lady Imogen Westham. He seemed to be meeting her more and more frequently at various social gatherings and discovered that he liked the special effort she always made to keep him amused and entertained. It was a novel experience for him to find this in a woman of Lady Imogen's refinement and accomplishments instead of in just another schoolroom chit out for the best offer she could wangle. He was now looking forward to the excursion to Richmond as an opportunity to examine Lady Imogen in the daylight and see if she fared as well under the revealing glare of the sun as in the softening glow of candlelight.

But business always came before pleasure, and even on that Sunday morning Worthing intended to finish at least two hours of work before it came time to leave. The loss of the *Prosperity* was still bothering him; Lord Ingram had turned up nothing that indicated it was more than a lucky shot on the part of the French, but now another ship, the *Wayward Lady,* was delayed in reporting and Worthing feared the worst. He wished to go over the requisition sheets for the *Lady* in case of any possible disaster, and there were also the final arrangements to be made for the two ships sailing during the next week.

He was surprised to find Miss Stone already busy at her desk in the cubbyhole off the library. When she saw him she hastily swept some cards into a drawer as she bid him good morning.

"Good morning, Stone," he said pleasantly. "It is encouraging to see you already at work this fine Sunday morning. What is it that you are being so secretive about?"

"Nothing at all," she replied airily. Then, picking up a sheaf of papers, she said, "These are ready for your approval before submission to the Secretary."

He glanced over the sheets, neatly listed with required supplies and columns of figures indicating amount and cost. Knowing that the totals were doubtless accurate, he initialed them quickly and handed them back to Christabel.

"Your efficiency is commendable as always, but you have yet to answer my question."

"What question was that?" she asked innocently.

For the briefest moment Worthing wondered if Stone's secrecy had anything to do with the loss of the ship, but he dismissed the notion instantly as the product of a too vivid imagination and too suspicious nature, especially after noting the mischievous look on her face.

"What was it that you hid away in your drawer as I came in?" he asked slowly, with only the barest hint of impatience.

Christabel grinned. "Curiosity killed the cat."

"Stone!" he warned.

"My, aren't we pettish today," she chided, but pulled open the drawer and showed him the cards she had been labeling. "I was merely working on the seating arrangements for the dinner party to be held before the ball," she explained. "I thought you would not care to be reminded of it, you always seem to become irritated by any mention of it."

"Not so!" he protested untruthfully. "I have nothing but the keenest interest in all such social gatherings." He ignored her quizzically raised eyebrow. "Have you placed me in a good position at the table?"

"You are at the head, is that not good enough?"

"But who are to be my dinner companions? You know I cannot bear idle chitchat and if I find you have placed me next to someone like Miss Hopkins, I will find a way to repay you."

Christabel laughed. "Your threats reduce me to a quivering mass of jelly. I have placed Lady Imogen Westham on your one side and Lucy Altamont on your other, and since Sir Harvey Summering is on *her* other side, I doubt she will claim much of your attention. Does that meet with your approval?"

"I suppose so," he said, vaguely disappointed.

"If you do not like it, it can be easily changed," she offered, sensing his disapproval. "Although I may have to do some juggling."

"In that case, I had hoped that *you* would sit on my other side," Worthing said, "or I am likely to have an overdose of Lady Imogen that evening."

Christabel pushed her spectacles up with one finger and regarded him pointedly. "Lady Imogen would hardly think that an encouraging statement, although I do agree with the possibility."

"Do you indeed? I would not mind too much if you would take a leaf from her book and make more of an effort to keep me in good temper."

"How inutterably boring." She laid the cards out on the desk before her. "I could move Miss Altamont to Sir Harvey's other side and myself to her original place. But won't people think it odd for me to sit so near the head? I had planned to sit among the War Office contingent to keep them amused, but I suppose I can move some of them up, too, and Sir Harvey down further. But now I must move the duke of Duxton, for I don't think I should care to sit across from him." She moved the cards around as she spoke.

"Dammit, Stone, it cannot be as complicated as all that. In another moment I will suggest you have a table all to yourself by the window, leaving me to my dinner in peace."

"Lady Imogen would not care for *that,* it would make me far too conspicuous and in danger of upstaging her. Why do we not put the two of you at a table alone; then you can have a lovely tête-à-tête with no one on your other side."

He made a sound approaching a growl. "Do as you please."

"I intend to," she said pleasantly. "And while we are on the subject, may I remind you that you have a fitting for your costume tomorrow at noon?" She laughed to herself as his only reply was an expressive shrug of his shoulders.

They did manage to get a full two hours of work completed before it came time for Worthing to change his clothes for the afternoon's expedition. He was awaiting his sister-in-law in the hallway, to drive with her to Duxton House and then on to Richmond, when Saunders handed him a dispatch that had just been delivered.

"This came while you were dressing, sir," he said.

Worthing tore it open, read it quickly and then exclaimed "Damn!" very loudly several times. He turned quickly and pulled the library door open, bellowing up the stairs, "Stone! Come down here immediately! Damnation!"

Christabel, up in the nursery helping Mrs. Drake with Richard, heard the sound of his voice over two flights of stairs, and with a brief alarmed glance at Mrs. Drake, immediately ran down to see what was wanted.

Worthing handed her the dispatch. "The *Wayward Lady* has been taken. Sunk in enemy waters nearly a week ago, the entire crew taken prisoner. Damn!" He loosened his cravat and took his place behind the desk. "That settles it. I will not be going on this deuced picnic after all."

"There is no need for you to remain behind," Christabel said. "I know what must be done. You go on ahead and we can finish when you return."

"Nonsense. Why should we both miss our little outing? I will stay here and you go on ahead."

"But I was not invited on the picnic anyway. I had planned to spend a quiet day reading in my room."

Worthing was surprised. "I had assumed all along that you were coming with us. But never mind, we'll *both* stay behind and work. This is much more important than any picnic."

But when Lady Fenworth was informed of this decision a few minutes later, she seemed to have decidedly different ideas on the matter.

"But, Justin, you *promised,*" she appealed to him plaintively. "You wrote the engagement in your diary a month ago—I saw you do it. We put it off until today just for you."

"I am sorry, Phoebe, but there is no help for it." He glanced toward Christabel for support, but she was wisely looking out the window, seemingly oblivious to the discussion at hand.

Phoebe's face screwed up as she made a valiant

effort not to cry, for she did not wish to spoil her appearance for Lord Ingram. "But, Justin, I don't understand—how can the loss of a ship thousands of miles away give you more work to do *now?* There is nothing you can do about it, is there?"

"No," he admitted, then explained as patiently as he could, "but we must determine what supplies the ship was carrying so that we can send replacements immediately. We have to rearrange everything, and Stone and I must go through all the requisition sheets to see how this can best be done." Even as he explained this to her he groaned inwardly at the tedium of the task, which they had already performed once before, and which made that morning's work quite useless.

Suddenly Phoebe brightened. "But, Justin, if it is just going through lists, can't you bring them along? You and Stoney can work on them in the carriage—I wouldn't mind. And then you will still be able to join us, and Stoney will, too, which she wouldn't have before. I am sure Lady Imogen won't mind." She smiled sunnily at the end of this as she realized she had come up with a full-fledged Plan.

"That is not a bad idea," Christabel put in. "I am willing to go along with it if you are." Lady Fenworth smiled at her gratefully for her support.

Worthing sighed deeply and paused for a moment, head in hands. A number of things went through his head, including the thought that the picnic now seemed even more attractive compared to the boring mindlessness of the task ahead.

He lifted his head slowly. "Very well, Phoebe," he said, "but I am afraid you will have to delay the journey for about half an hour while we gather the materials we need." He consulted his watch. "Let us say we will leave at half past twelve."

Phoebe was delighted with this decision and went happily up to the drawing room to write Lady Imogen a brief note informing her of the change in plans.

Lady Imogen, on the other hand, was definitely not delighted with this news. She had made careful arrangements beforehand so she would be assured of riding in the same carriage as Worthing, while Lady Fenworth and her son shared a second carriage with Mary Hopkins, and Lucy Altamont rode in Sir Harvey's phaeton. With the addition of Miss Stone to the party, Lady Imogen found she was expected to share a carriage with both other ladies and the young earl, since Worthing and Miss Stone needed a carriage all to themselves. She wished now that she had chosen to ride, as her brother and Mr. Waters, the other member of the party, were doing, but while she could have easily called for her horse, this would have necessitated her changing into a riding habit, and that she would not do. She had had a costume made especially for the occasion, an ensemble modeled after a Balkan peasant's garb, with a full red skirt and white blouse, gaily embroidered. Rather than take this off she felt she would make the best of the situation, arranging things more to her liking at the picnic itself.

But here again she was thwarted. Once they were settled at Richmond, with blankets spread upon the ground—for it was a truly rustic affair despite the complaints of several of the gentlemen who would have preferred sitting around tables in the inn—she once again found herself separated from Worthing. In her efforts to avoid the hen-witted Miss Hopkins, she had somehow ended up in what might otherwise have been a very promising tête-à-tête between Miss Altamont and Sir Harvey but for her presence. Her brother and his friend Percy Waters were busy entertaining Richard, to the great delight of his mother, and Mr. Worthing and his frightfully unattractive secretary were still pouring over papers, quite oblivious to the rest of the company. Somehow, though, Lady Imogen was able to get through the meal with a reasonable amount of grace.

Finally, Sir Harvey stood up, and with Miss Altamont on one arm, he very kindly offered his other arm to Lady Imogen as they took a stroll around the park.

"No, thank you," she said, with her gracious smile that was always ready for such occasions no matter how put out she felt. "I prefer not to take exercise so soon after eating."

Sir Harvey was too polite to show his relief at this refusal, and after half-heartedly pressing her once more, he and Miss Altamont took off on their own.

Left alone, Lady Imogen decided that it was time for the party to re-form, so she stood up, brushed a few crumbs off her bright skirt and walked decidedly over to where Worthing sat.

"Come, come," she laughed, "this is no way to have a picnic."

"Ah, Lady Imogen," Worthing greeted her, "are you enjoying yourself?"

"A great deal more than you seem to be," she

said. "Remember, all work and no play makes Jack a dull boy."

"That observation has been made to me before," Worthing replied wryly, "but I do not consider myself dull, nor is my name Jack."

Lady Imogen quickly assured him, "I did not mean to say that you were dull, only that you might become so. You must admit that your heart does not seem to be in the enjoyment of our expedition. I propose that you leave your papers to come rowing with me. The water is so lovely today, and we have already engaged several boats for the occasion. I am sure Miss Stone can spare you." She favored Christabel, whom she had been ignoring until now, with a sour smile.

"But I thought you did not care to take exercise so soon after eating," Christabel remarked, smiling just as sourly.

Lady Imogen looked at her coldly. "You have sharp ears, Miss Stone. A very valuable trait in a governess, I am sure. Of course I did not wish to walk with the others, they so obviously wanted to be alone"—she flashed her smile—"but I am persuaded exercise would be beneficial to you, Mr. Worthing, and there are those of us who are interested in your continued health." She lowered her eyelids coyly.

Worthing gave Christabel an amused wink which said as well as words, "You see, *this* is the way to keep me in good temper."

Aloud he said, "That sounds a splendid idea, Lady Imogen. And since you have engaged several boats, why don't we make a party of it? I think Richard has never been in a rowing boat." He caught Lady Fenworth's eye and beckoned to her, and in a few minutes most of the party was heading toward the landing, leaving Christabel behind with Mrs. Drake and the few other servants who were busy clearing away the remains of the meal.

"I reckon that piece of work thinks she has caught Master Justin hook, line and sinker," Mrs. Drake observed to Christabel.

"She would make him a suitable wife," Christabel offered without much conviction.

"I daresay she would, if that's all he wants. But there's suitable and there's suitable. If you ask me, she bears too close a resemblance to a certain other young woman who would be best forgotten."

"Does she indeed?" Christabel asked, her interest sparking. "Do you mean the one Mr. Worthing was in love with years ago?"

"In love with," Mrs. Drake snorted. "Nay, I think not. But there's things other than love that will lead a man to folly. I only hope Master Justin has learned from his past mistake. There's no heart in a woman like that; plenty of show, but no heart."

Christabel nodded. "But perhaps he is not seeking a heart."

"Oh, he is all right, if he only had the sense to know it, but since that old affair, he has built a wall around himself. You see, I know Master Justin through and through, and I also know that if it's suitable he wants, he need look no further than his own house."

"What do you mean?"

"What do I mean? Bless the child! I mean you."

"Me?" Christabel exclaimed, flustered. "But you are mistaken. Mr. Worthing has never thought of me in *that* regard, I assure you."

111

"No, that he hasn't," Mrs. Drake agreed regretfully. "It's where he and his brother were always the same—heads turned by a pretty face. But one day you will forget to paint your face and put on your spectacles, and maybe then he'll notice you as he should."

"I don't know what you are talking about," Christabel said coldly, turning away.

"Do you not? I've eyes in my head, haven't I? Who do you suppose it is what changes your pillow slips, finding them all streaked with yellow cream? But don't worry, my dear, your secret is safe with me. I'm sure you have your reasons for doing as you do, and no one would be happier than I to see you win him away from our fine Lady Imogen, with or without a disguise."

Fortunately, Christabel was spared from the further confusion and embarrassment Mrs. Drake's pronouncements were causing her by the reappearance of Lord Ingram.

"Well met, Miss Stone," he greeted her as soon as he was within earshot. "I seem to be odd man out, there was no room in the boat for me, so I had to leave my lady love in the questionable care of Percy Waters." He sprawled out casually on the blanket beside her, while Mrs. Drake unobtrusively withdrew.

"What a shame," Christabel said, smiling.

"Not at all. Even on these glassy waters I am bound to become seasick. And this gives us the perfect opportunity to become better acquainted. You have become much admired in government circles, Miss Stone, and to claim friendship with you will undoubtedly increase my own estimation in the eyes of my superiors."

Get Your
Coventry Romances
Home Subscription NOW

And Get These
4 Best-Selling Novels
FREE!

You give a lot of love in your life. Let Coventry give you a little old-fashioned romance.

HELENE
Discovers true adventure, friendship, love, and intrigue after turning her back on her refined upbringing and a flurry of society men she couldn't respect...

LUCY
War and scandal make two brothers the objects of her love and hate. But, shockingly, not the way she expected...

LUCIA
Loves one man but marries another to escape a spiteful stepsister...

LACEY
Beautiful, spirited, and wealthy, she runs away and hides her identity to find true love...

Lacey, Lucia, Helene, Lucy...these are some of the memorable women who come alive in the pages of Coventry Romances. Historical love stories that, month after month, make you feel the elegance and grandeur of another time and place. And now, without leaving your home, you can share in this special kind of romance!

The Coventry home subscription plan is the easiest and most convenient way to get every one of the exciting Coventry Romances! You'll be sure not to miss any of these great historical romances, and you won't even have to go out looking for them.

"In that case, I feel I should charge a fee for my acquaintance," Christabel said, easily falling in with his bantering tones.

"Name your price, Miss Stone. I will gladly pay it."

"High honor indeed, from one who is always complaining of having pockets to let."

"Do I complain so? But never fear, this month I can pay any price you name, for I have come into a windfall."

"Then I should pay for *your* acquaintance, you who have learned to draw water from a stone."

"That stone being my father, I presume, and not your esteemed self."

Christabel laughed. "Certainly not I! All my acquaintances are in arrears in their payments."

"Let me not be counted among them," Lord Ingram said, and removing the small pearl stickpin from his cravat, he solemnly held it out to her. "Take this on account, Miss Stone."

Christabel laughed uncertainly, not knowing whether he was serious or not. "Oh, I could not, sir, my fees are not so high."

"But I wish to claim your acquaintance for a good long time. It is but a trifle and will look well on the bodice of your gown where no other ornament disturbs the vast expanse of black."

He continued to hold it out to her, so she had no choice but to take it and pin it to her bodice as instructed. "I hope this token of friendship will not invoke your sister's displeasure. She does not care for me overmuch, I fear."

"Then more fool her, say I. But there is another member of my family who has nothing but the

113

highest regard for you, and he would not be ashamed to see you wearing my token."

"Indeed?" Christabel murmured indistinctly; she knew he referred to the duke.

"Indeed," Lord Ingram said firmly. "I am sure he would like to hire you away from Worthing if he could, and I know he regards your efficiency as far superior to mine." He gave a short, rueful laugh. "He is right there, of course, for I am in the wrong profession. There are those in another profession who do not take my talents so lightly, but it is out of the question for me to enter *that* field seriously. My aunt, you see, married an actor and since then, the Pater has had no use for the lot of them."

"Indeed?" Christabel murmured again. She was grateful Lord Ingram could not see her face; fortunately he was now reclining, his hands behind his head, gazing at the sky.

"It is the bane of a younger son's existence that he must enter a profession at all," he continued absently. "What would I not give for some of my brother's ambition. He has no such obligation as I, and yet he serves his time in the army, leading troops on the Peninsula when he could be home, enjoying his status as heir to the coronet. There is no justice in the world, Miss Stone." He rambled on in this vein for a while longer, but beyond an appropriate murmur here and there Christabel had ceased to pay much attention to him, finding her own mind wandering to the implications of her recent conversation with Mrs. Drake.

They were interrupted by some very loud screams from the direction of the river. Lord

Ingram immediately leapt up, and offering his hand to Christabel to help her rise, said, "It sounds as though there has been an accident. Let us go see."

One of the grooms came running up to them. "Mr. Worthing's boat has gone over!" he yelled breathlessly. "They're all as wet as drowned rats!"

Chapter Eight

Mrs. Drake, with great presence of mind, immediately began gathering blankets from the ground. Christabel helped her and they walked quickly down to the river to see what had happened.

Lady Imogen was sitting in a miserable, wet heap on the boat landing. The colorful embroidery in her peasant blouse had run onto the white fabric, so that she was covered with messy red and blue blotches. Her hair hung wetly down her back, and the expression on her face was not so much fright as pure fury. Mrs. Drake quickly threw a blanket across her shoulders, while Lady Imogen complained loudly that it was dirty and covered with leaves and grass.

Meanwhile Richard, also quite wet, saw Christabel and ran up to her, crowing delightedly, "We all went bathing! I saw a sea monster and then we went bathing!"

Christabel wrapped a blanket around him and looked up at Worthing, who had come up behind him.

"Are the others all right?" she asked.

"Yes," he said, taking another blanket and rubbing himself vigorously with it. "Here they are now. I'll look after Richard, Stone, I think Lady Fenworth needs you."

Phoebe indeed needed Stone, for while the second boat had escaped harm and she was quite dry otherwise, her face was wet with the tears that had begun as soon as she saw her darling Dickie in the water. There was a great deal of difficulty in plucking her out of the boat without mishap as Mr. Waters handed her to Lord Ingram while Miss Hopkins tried to steady the swaying boat.

Once on dry land Phoebe had half a dozen comforters, all of them assuring her that Richard was quite safe. This she would not believe until she held her son in her arms and smothered him with kisses, which he accepted with uneasy grace as he tried to tell her of the sea monster he had fought. Miss Altamont and Sir Harvey, returning from their walk, also came up to form part of the throng.

In all this, Lady Imogen had been forgotten at the end of the dock, and her face was by now almost black with fury. Christabel was the only one to notice her and quickly went up to her with another blanket.

"Are you all right, your ladyship?" she asked kindly, her sympathy for her cousin's condition overriding her usual antipathy.

117

"I will strangle that wretched child," Lady Imogen fumed. "Do not put that blanket on me, Stone, it is quite filthy!"

Christabel dutifully shook the blanket out, for it was indeed covered with bits of grass, then wrapped it around Lady Imogen's shoulders. Despite these efforts, she was now shivering quite violently, both with chill and rage.

"That *beastly* little boy," she was muttering, more to herself, "why could he not have remained with his mother? Look at my dress, it is quite ruined. *Stop* it, Stone, I will dry my own hair. Look at the fuss they are making over that little monster. Does no one care about *me?*"

"Hush, Lady Imogen, you will make yourself ill. Come, I'll take you up to the inn where we can find some dry clothes for you."

"It is your fault, Stone. You should have been looking after him. No one invited you on this wretched picnic anyway, I certainly did not want you here. Oh, my beautiful skirt, it is a complete ruin."

Christabel did not pause to argue with her, but started toward the nearby inn, where the rest of the company was now headed.

"Quite an adventure, eh, Lady Im?" Percy Waters came to walk beside them. "Your brother and I thought we might do a piece on it. 'Disaster at Richmond,' or 'The Wreck of the Bluebell,' something like that."

Lady Imogen retained a stony silence at this sally.

"It's a miracle we didn't go down, too," Percy continued cheerfully. "Lady Fen nearly jumped out of the boat when she saw the little chap go

118

under. All I could do to hold her back. Could do a piece on that, I suppose—'Mother Love Takes a Dive.' " He chuckled.

"Oh, do shut up, Percy, you are the most incredible bore," Lady Imogen told him cuttingly, and he went away with an injured expression to seek out Lord Ingram with another idea for a piece entitled "Beauty Disarranged."

Once at the inn, the wet members of the party were bundled off to find dry clothes, while the others engaged a private parlor and ordered a bowl of punch. Christabel left Lady Imogen when she cried impatiently that she was quite capable of seeing to herself, and instead took her place at Lady Fenworth's side, offering her a glass of punch to calm her frazzled nerves.

"I think it was the most frightening moment of my life," Phoebe was saying. "I should have kept him in the boat with me and let Mary go with Justin and Imogen. I shall never forgive myself."

Miss Hopkins, who was sitting inconspicuously in a corner of the room, did not offer the opinion that Lady Imogen would have certainly objected to such an arrangement. She was a quiet girl whose chief virtue was the fact that she generally held her tongue.

"I must say, Sir Harvey and I had quite a fright when we saw them all being pulled out of the water," Miss Altamont offered. "I don't care to go rowing myself. I had a cousin once who was drowned in a yacht and it has quite put me off the notion of boating forever."

Sir Harvey offered a similar tale, and Percy Waters declared that he would write a piece on it, if Lord Ingram would help him find a rhyme for yacht. They all succeeded so well in removing Lady Fenworth's mind from the recent near disaster to her son that she was almost surprised to see him come bounding in, dressed in a man's shirt that reached nearly to the floor.

"Look, Mama!" he cried, "I'm dressed just like an old Greek, isn't that right, Stoney?"

Christabel laughed. "Close enough, Richard."

Worthing came in shortly thereafter, and having been able to borrow some clothes from another gentleman who was staying at the inn, was dressed rather more respectably than his nephew. The same could not be said of Lady Imogen, who entered wearing a rather shapeless garment of coarse linsey-woolsey, and as she helped herself to a glass of punch, she couldn't help but notice Richard's frank stare.

"Has your governess not taught you that it is rude to stare?" she asked dauntingly. She made sure that her voice could be heard by Christabel, who quickly came up to remove Richard from Lady Imogen's presence, bringing him over to join Miss Hopkins in the corner.

"Are you quite all right, Lady Imogen?" Worthing asked her solicitously. "I apologize for my nephew's unruly behavior."

"And so you should," Lady Imogen replied sharply. "He is totally undisciplined and it is disgraceful that he is not being punished at this very moment."

Worthing was surprised by the cold fury behind her words. He was well used to sharp rejoinders from his secretary, but they were always accompanied with a hint of laughter to soften the cutting words. There was nothing soft behind Lady Imogen's remark.

"I assure you, Madam, that my nephew will be dealt with at the proper time and place," he answered formally, and forbore adding that he thought it was no business of hers.

Something in his tone brought Lady Imogen back to herself and she forced a smile. "I did not mean to sound critical, it is only that I am not used to being thrown in the river."

"No, of course not," Worthing agreed warmly. "It is not a usual occupation for a lady."

She laughed wanly and took another sip of punch before Worthing led her to a seat by the fireplace, where Percy Waters was extemporizing on the theme of shipwrecks in rhymed iambic pentameter.

The party broke up soon afterward, the spirits of all—excepting perhaps Mr. Waters—having been thoroughly dampened by the near disaster. Worthing, having suffered not at all from his dunking, was nonetheless left with a vague uneasiness, stemming from Lady Imogen's revelation of a side to her nature he had not previously known to exist. It seemed she was possessed of quite as violent a temper as his own, and he was still not certain whether he should regard this as an asset in one he could quite possibly make his wife. But he was convinced that he should make no commitment to the lady yet, where his heart was not involved, his head could most certainly afford to wait.

As the several weeks until the ball passed, only one clue was found regarding any wrongdoing behind the fate of the two lost ships. Lord Ingram turned up a piece of information indicating that a Spanish-looking man had been seen twice in Dover at the appropriate times. Beyond this there was nothing to go on except Worthing's increasing suspicion that if someone were leaking information, it had to be someone in the War Office. Confiding this suspicion only to Christabel, he went so far as to prepare with her a false supply list, to be planted whenever it seemed appropriate. How this was to lead to disclosure of the traitor he was not sure, but knew he had to do something besides sit and twiddle his thumbs.

Christabel had no chance to visit her stepmother again until the day before the ball, when she went to the theater to pick up the costume she was borrowing. After a delighted exchange of greetings, Alexis noticed the pearl stickpin Christabel wore on her bodice.

"It was a gift from my cousin," she said proudly. "We have become great friends, you know."

Alexis eyed the pin warily. "You mean Lord Ingram, I presume, and not Lady Imogen." Christabel nodded. "Myself, I do not care for him too much. He seems a rackety sort of fellow. He is seeing one of the girls here and always reciting the most frightful doggerel to her. Of course, she loves it."

"You sound like Mr. Worthing. He does not approve of Ingram, either. I will admit that he is rather fanciful, but then he is so good-looking and charming one can forgive him that."

Alexis looked at her sharply. "I hope you are not developing a *tendre* for this fellow, Chris. I fear it would not be at all suitable."

Christabel laughed. "No, not at all. Ingram is interested in Lady Fenworth and I think they would make quite a good pair. No, Alex, you know I am not interested in any man *that* way."

Alexis seemed relieved by this, but not convinced. "And tell me," she said, "is your costume quite all right? I take it Mr. Worthing is attending this ball as Henry VIII."

"Yes, he is, but how did you guess that?"

"It was not difficult, my dear, once I saw your costume." No, Alexis was not at all convinced of Christabel's disinterest in men, but felt she could rest easy as far as Lord Ingram was concerned.

They chatted a while longer until Alexis received the signal that it was nearly time to go on stage. Christabel kissed her goodbye and was walking down the corridor to the side exit, the costume in a box under her arm, when from around the corner she heard what sounded like the duke of Duxton speaking to someone with a Spanish accent. She stopped short, wondering why Alexis had not mentioned he was to visit her that night; if she were still seeing him to promote Christabel's interests, why hadn't she said so?

Christabel debated whether she should turn the corner and greet the duke, but then decided it would be better not to. If he saw her there, he might make the connection between her and Alexis and realize who she really was—then her position and the whole new life she was building for herself would be gone. So instead, she hung back, waiting for him to walk on so that she might make her exit unnoticed, but meanwhile from where she was she could not help but overhear some of the conversation. She knew the other man must be

Santanos, the theater manager whom Alexis so despised, and it seemed as though the two men were trying to strike some kind of bargain.

"Four thousand should be more than enough," the duke was saying. "I cannot see how you would need more than that."

"But most noble Señor, I don't think you understand all that is required. It is a most complicated undertaking." The Spaniard's voice was smooth and confident.

"Very well," the duke said, capitulating. "Forty-five hundred and that is my final offer."

"That should do very nicely, Señor Duke."

"I will write you a check for one thousand now—that should be enough for you to go on with."

"Oh, please, only cash, Señor Duke. So much more convenient."

"Very well," the duke said grudgingly. "But I haven't any cash with me now. I had an unfortunate accident today and was relieved of my possessions. I will bring it tomorrow and the rest next week."

Christabel peeped cautiously around the corner, to see them shaking hands on the matter, then drew back quickly as the duke seemed to look in her direction.

It wasn't until much later that the full weight of what she had heard hit her, and even then she wasn't sure what she was thinking could be correct. She decided she would do some research of her own before she presented Worthing with this interesting information.

Chapter Nine

"No further, I beg you! I cannot breathe! I am suffocating! I cannot bear any more!"

"Hold still, your ladyship, we are almost finished," Dorcas told her sharply. She and Christabel were attempting to lace Lady Fenworth into her sixteenth-century corset, a project which demanded not only determination but also some brute strength.

"It has been made too tight," Lady Fenworth said faintly, holding on to the bedpost for support as the laces were pulled. "I am certain she measured me incorrectly."

"Not so, your ladyship," Dorcas replied, "it is just that you have got out of the habit of wearing a corset. Do you not remember how it was before the young earl was born?"

"It was not nearly so bad as this," Phoebe pouted. "I will be unable to eat a thing tonight, for there certainly is no room for it. And we ordered all those lobster patties *especially*."

"There!" Christabel exclaimed as the two edges of the corset finally met in the middle of Lady Fenworth's back.

Phoebe let go of the bedpost and tried to take a deep breath but was unsuccessful. "It is *definitely* too tight, I can barely catch my breath."

"Nonsense!" Dorcas declared. "If it was any looser, the gown would not go over it."

Phoebe gave a pitiful little sigh. "It is like being enclosed between two pieces of wood. I don't see why my dressmaker had to be *quite* so authentic."

"Perhaps you should have been Queen Guinevere, your ladyship," Christabel suggested. "She is always represented as wearing loose, flowing gowns and I am sure Lord Ingram would have been pleased to dress as Sir Lancelot."

"It is too late now," Phoebe said woefully as Dorcas slipped the heavy gown over her head. After considerable arrangement she was finally able to view herself in the looking glass and despite her discomfort was pleased with what she saw.

"What do you think, Stoney?"

"Splendid!" Christabel declared truthfully. "You will put everyone else to shame."

Phoebe turned her large brown eyes to Dorcas for confirmation of this pronouncement.

Dorcas nodded and said, "You'll do, your ladyship."

She turned once more to the glass, giggling with sudden pleasure. "Yes, I suppose it does look well on me, but it seems frightfully silly to have spent hundreds of pounds just so I could be squeezed to

126

death by this frightful thing." She thumped the front of the gown, making a sound like the knocking of a door. "What is it called again, Stoney?"

"A stomacher," Christabel replied. "But, your ladyship, do not feel that your money is all wasted. You will make a sensation tonight, and tomorrow you can remove all the pearls and make them into a necklace."

"I already have a pearl necklace," Phoebe said, missing the irony in Christabel's voice. "Where is it? Dorcas, I must not forget to put it on."

Seeing that her assistance was no longer required, Christabel took her leave. "If you will excuse me, your ladyship, I will go now and put on my own costume and make sure Lord Fenworth is ready."

"Thank you, Stoney, and do remind Mrs. Drake that I want Dickie in the drawing room *before* dinner, because after dinner we will go straight into the ballroom."

Christabel found Richard dressed and, like his mother, complaining about the discomfort of his costume. She conveyed Lady Fenworth's message to Mrs. Drake, who said she'd already been told that a thousand times, and then went to change into her own unremarkable costume.

The identity she would assume had been suggested to her by Lady Fenworth, but Christabel knew quite well that the idea had originated with Lady Imogen. The costume consisted simply of a black gown with an imitation stomacher sewn onto the front and a large black domino. She changed into it quickly, applied another coating of powder to her hair where it had flaked off and patted some more yellowish cream on her face to retain

127

her falsely sallow complexion. Then, with a quick, sly glance at the costume she would don later on, she went downstairs to the library to check on some unfinished business there.

Justin Worthing felt extremely silly as Henry VIII. His coat, with its well-padded shoulders, was too tight in the arms and he felt certain it would split down the middle of the back as soon as he began to dance. Worse than that, though, was the fact that it boasted no pocket wherein he could carry his watch, and he found himself to be at a severe disadvantage without his timepiece.

Despite these problems, he was dressed early and so, having a few minutes to spare, went down to the library to make a few notes for another report. There he found Christabel, sitting at his desk, looking through some papers.

"Stone," he said, a note of surprise in his voice, "should you not be dressing for the ball? The guests will be arriving for dinner at any moment."

"Mr. Worthing," she said, jumping up quickly from his chair. "I regret to inform you that this *is* my costume." With an almost unnoticed movement she hid a paper in the folds of her gown and then looked him over carefully. "Don't you look smart!" she exclaimed. "But I think there is something not quite right about it." She stood up and circled around him, trying to put her finger on just what was wrong with his elegant attire. "I know what it is! You are far too *thin*, Mr. Worthing. I have never before seen such a thin Henry VIII."

Worthing made a sound something like a growl. "The damn fool made a great padded waistcoat to wear with it, but I was afraid it would be too warm and the coat is tight enough as it is." He mumbled something else under his breath that sounded like "prancing jackanapes."

"You are probably right," Christabel said sympathetically. "I still fear we have invited far more people than the ballroom will hold, and there is bound to be a terrible crush."

Worthing nodded as he reached for his watch and was frustrated. "Blast," he muttered, and then caught the twinkle in Christabel's eye and chuckled. "It must be nearly a quarter to eight," he said, "are you certain you do not need to change?" He gave her plain black dress a critical gaze.

"Quite certain," Christabel replied. "The only other addition to my costume is a black domino, which I will put on after dinner."

"But whom are you supposed to represent?"

"Isn't it obvious? I am Queen Elizabeth's nursemaid, or Edward IV's nursemaid—I suppose it doesn't really matter which. I believe it was Lady Imogen's idea."

"And is that paper you are trying to hide from me part of the ensemble? Perhaps it is the missive that will rob Mary, Queen of Scots of her head?"

She laughed guiltily. "No, it is merely the result of some research I have undertaken." A small shadow passed over her face, but was gone instantly as she forced a bright laugh. "But it is not important now," she said, as she walked over to place it on her own desk. "We can discuss it tomorrow. Tonight is for amusement only."

"If you find it amusing to play host to half of London dressed as silly schoolchildren, with fond mamas waiting in the wings in hopes that under the security of masks I will perform some minor indiscretion and so be trapped into a proposal of marriage."

"I fear you flatter yourself. Surely there is no danger of *that*."

"On the contrary, Stone, you underestimate me. I have it on good authority that I am considered quite a catch. I'll wager there will be more than one young lady dressed as Ann Boleyn tonight."

"Then make yourself easy, sire," Christabel said, twinkling. "Lady Imogen is among them and I am sure she will keep all pretenders at bay."

"As long as my nephew does not contrive to drop her in the fishpond tonight. I have observed that Lady Imogen's temper suffers considerably from a wetting."

"And who can blame her?" Christabel said, surprised to find herself actually taking her cousin's part.

Worthing cocked an eyebrow at her, surprised for the same reason. "Do not tell me that you have decided to promote Lady Imogen's suit?"

"No, indeed, but in the interest of fairness it is only right to point out that what happened at Richmond was quite out of the ordinary and enough to make anyone lose her temper. *I* certainly should have."

"I have absolutely no doubt as to *that*," Worthing assured her.

Christabel merely said, "Hmmm," then gave him an old fashioned curtsy. "If you will excuse me, sire, I think I had better go and look after my queen, or whatever it is that nursemaids do."

Lady Fenworth was indeed in need of Christabel's help, for she was finding it extremely awkward to maneuver in the wide panniers and heavy, flowing train that were also part of her costume.

"However am I to dance in this, Stoney?" she asked in a small, plaintive voice as Christabel escorted her into the drawing room. "I can barely *walk*."

"I think, my lady, that the train can be removed," Christabel said helpfully.

"But it is so pretty!"

"Yes, but it is very heavy, as you have noticed, and I think you would manage better without it after dinner."

"Of course, you are right," Phoebe agreed humbly.

Worthing joined them a few minutes later and it was not long before the two dozen dinner guests began to arrive.

Lord Ingram Westham was effusive over Lady Fenworth's attire, and immediately began reciting a poem he had composed especially for the occasion. Lady Fenworth blushed delicately at this attention and said several times, "Please, Ingram," and "No more, my lord."

He finished with a flourish, speading his cape on the floor before her, saying gallantly, "Sir Walter Raleigh is always at your service, Majesty, ever your slave."

Phoebe giggled uncertainly, then realized she was neglecting her other guests. She turned to greet a new arrival who was speaking to Justin, a very handsome man, she thought vaguely, with something so familiar about him that she wondered if they had met before, although she could not remember such an occasion.

131

Lord Ingram cleared up her confusion immediately by introducing her to his father, the duke of Duxton.

Lady Fenworth's first impression was that he did not seem to be the tyrant his son and daughter made him out to be, and as he bent over her hand and gave her a pretty compliment—not a tenth as effusive as his son's, but at least she understood every word—she found herself wondering how Lady Imogen could speak of him in such disparaging terms.

"And who are you dressed as?" she asked him.

"I fear, my lady, that as I left my tailor's yesterday with my costume safely tucked under my arm, I was accosted by footpads and relieved of all that was in my possession at the time. And so you see me as I am."

"That's a Banbury Tale if ever I heard one, Duxton," Worthing put in. "Admit that you did not wish to make a fool of yourself like the rest of us."

"On the contrary, Worthing, it is most unfortunately true," the duke replied. "In fact, it has led me to take precautions against a similar incident in the future. But I will admit I am not too broken up over the loss of my costume, I have a decided aversion to fancy dress."

"Well, who hasn't? I haven't even a place to put my watch in this outlandish coat."

Lady Fenworth was about to agree with them wholeheartedly, for her corset was pinching most dreadfully, but Lord Ingram spoke up first,

"You gentlemen have no spirit of romance," he said. "It should at least give you a sense of history to dress as our forefathers did."

"And so it would had they not such unusual taste," Worthing said.

"In fifty years they will doubtless say the same of us," Lord Ingram pointed out.

"You'll have to agree with him there!" Duxton declared heartily.

"You see, even my father agrees with me, so there must be some truth in what I say." The three men laughed and Lady Fenworth joined in tentatively, uncertain where the joke lay.

Meanwhile, Lady Imogen, after a short greeting from Mr. Worthing, had wandered off and found herself standing next to Christabel.

"Miss Stone," Lady Imogen said in her most condescending manner, "why aren't you in fancy dress like all the rest? Surely you have no excuse such as my father's." She knew very well that Christabel was in costume and also whom she was supposed to represent.

"Oh, but I am," Christabel replied sweetly, "I am dressed as Anne Boleyn's prison wardress. Couldn't you tell?"

Lady Imogen's smile soured. "Indeed? How amusing. And did Anne Boleyn's prison wardress have eczema, too?"

She referred, Christabel knew, to the faint sprinkling of powder that had fallen to her shoulders from her hair. "There is no telling what one might pick up in a prison, Lady Imogen. I shouldn't be at all surprised if Anne Boleyn had caught it herself—toward the end, that is."

Lady Imogen gave an unamused little laugh, then noticed Mrs. Drake entering with the young earl in tow. "Ah, here is your little charge now, Miss Stone. Tell me, how does he get on in his studies? Have you cured his fancy for hunting sea monsters?"

"You forget, Lady Imogen, that I am not Lord Fenworth's governess but Mr. Worthing's secretary."

"Still?" Lady Imogen said with an air of great surprise. "However does he get any of his work done?" But before Christabel could retort to this, Lady Imogen sailed over to stand next to Worthing and they listened to her brother recite another poem, this time in honor of Lord Fenworth. She even swallowed her aversion to little Dickie, who was valiantly holding up under his mother's fond embraces, to make a flattering remark about his costume. She did this partly to make amends for her show of temper at Richmond and partly to give Worthing an opening for a similar remark about her own gown.

In this she was to be disappointed until much later, when dinner was nearly over and Worthing, in his faltering efforts at small talk, had made every possible remark about the weather there was to make. Finally exhausting this subject, Worthing did manage to say that Lady Imogen's pearls were very fine. This was all the opening she needed, and she went on to point out the many other fine details her costume boasted, although she admitted that she simply could not bring herself to have an extra finger sewn onto her glove.

"I *had* thought it would be a most authentic touch," she said with a light laugh, "but it was simply too vulgar to carry out."

At this Worthing remarked something to the effect that it was nothing to lose her head over, which prompted a loud, delighted outburst of laughter from her, and she promptly repeated the remark to the gentleman seated on her other side, who was to be only the first to hear the repetition of the joke.

Christabel, seated on Worthing's other side, leaned over slightly to say in his ear, "You might also have mentioned something about how be-*witch*ing she looks."

"I wish I had thought of that!" he exclaimed. "I will reserve it for later when we dance together."

Lady Imogen was not quite so pleased with her chosen disguise when the rest of the ball guests arrived later on and she discovered no fewer than three Anne Boleyns among them, all hopeful of attracting Mr. Worthing's notice, and one of whom had dared to wear a glove with the extra finger sewn on. Lady Imogen remarked to her brother, didn't he think Cynthia Bromley's costume vulgar in the extreme and not nearly so nice as her own?

"Nose out of joint, Imogen?" he asked. "I half expected a great many more Anne Boleyns than there are—after all, Worthing's a prime catch. Perhaps you should have come as another of his wives. Catherine of Aragon with the pox on her. Now *that* would have attracted attention."

"Oh, hush, you are dreadful," Lady Imogen said crossly, doubly annoyed as she recalled Miss Stone's remark about eczema. "I am only glad that I was present at dinner, so that even with my mask he knows who I am. Those other girls cannot hope to be identified."

"*I* know who they are, and *you* have recognized

135

them, so there is no reason to suppose Worthing cannot."

"Oh, do go away, Ingram," she said pettishly. "You are being thoroughly unpleasant tonight. I think your queen requires your attendance." She indicated Lady Fenworth, who was indeed beckoning to Lord Ingram as the first dance was about to begin.

"Ingram," Lady Fenworth said as he approached her. "I must dance the first dance with Justin, I hope you don't mind."

Lord Ingram did mind, since he supposed he was about to have that honor conferred upon himself, but he submitted with a good grace and, taking her hand in a courtly gesture, hoped that she might honor him with the first waltz.

Phoebe giggled in a manner totally incongruous with her costume and said, "Ingram, you do it all so *well.*"

"Practice, my lady," he said gravely. "I am ever practicing." Then he noticed another young lady of his acquaintance standing alone and went to secure her hand for the dance.

To Lady Imogen's extreme annoyance, Worthing did not dance the next dance with her either, but with Miss Bromley. It would not have consoled her any to know that Worthing had thought it *was* Lady Imogen he had approached—for their costumes were very like now that the masks had been donned. It was not until Miss Bromley's extra finger flapped against his hand as they were dancing that he realized his mistake, but by then it was too late.

Not easily defeated, Lady Imogen maneuvered her partner so that they finished the dance quite close to Worthing and Miss Bromley. She sent the unfortunate fellow to fetch her a glass of punch, and cast Worthing a few demure glances from her snapping black eyes, as she liked to hear them described, which he failed to notice.

"Lady Imogen, have you something in your eye?" Christabel asked suddenly, quite close to her ear.

"No, indeed," Lady Imogen replied, starting, for she had not noticed Miss Stone standing there.

"If you wish to dance with Mr. Worthing, I will tell him so," Christabel offered, the soul of helpfulness. "I don't believe he has noticed you are free."

"Thank you all the same, Miss Stone," Lady Imogen said coldly, "but I do not need an ambassadress. Especially one who cannot seem to find any partners of her own."

"I have partners aplenty, but I have chosen not to dance tonight, for Mr. Worthing is depending upon me to keep all the ministers of state engaged in conversation so they do not suddenly discover they are not enjoying themselves. By the way, I told him to tell you that you are quite bewitching, so be sure to laugh appropriately or he will be most dreadfully cut up."

Lady Imogen pointedly ignored this last remark and in a few moments had made her way to Worthing's side and was rewarded for her trouble when he seemed quite pleased to see her, indeed mentioned that he had been looking for her, and immediately asked her to dance. However, her pleasure in this occupation diminished sharply when the only remark he made to her, besides mentioning that it was frightfully hot, was that she looked bewitching. Lady Imogen could barely bring herself to smile appropriately as she had been instructed.

Later, she found herself once again at her brother's side.

"Miss Stone seems to be keeping the War Office contingent amused," he remarked conversationally, indicating the lady in question who was surrounded by a knot of men, most of whom, like the duke, wore only a domino over their usual evening clothes in concession to the fancy dress nature of the ball.

"Humph," was Lady Imogen's reply.

Lord Ingram looked at her quizzically. "I take it you are not fond of our Miss Stone."

"*Your* Miss Stone!" she exclaimed. "I did not know she had become common property."

"Why, she's almost a fixture by now," Lord Ingram said easily. "Some of the other ministers are actually considering finding female secretaries— much more secure than a man who is looking for advancement. But I doubt they'll find anyone like Stone. She's a very remarkable lady."

"I assume you use the term 'lady' loosely."

"Now, sis, cattiness doesn't become you," he admonished. "But cheer up, she seems to be leaving now." Miss Stone was indeed working her way to the door, wishing good-night to the gentlemen gathered around her.

"Not a moment too soon for my taste," Lady Imogen muttered under her breath.

"The Pater seems to be taken with our little Lady Fenworth," Lord Ingram remarked, watching as his father secured Lady Fenworth's hand for the next dance. "I am relieved; it will smooth the way for me. He made a positive fuss when she brought out the little brat before dinner."

"And I suppose what you did could not be called a fuss?" Lady Imogen asked him caustically.

Lord Ingram chuckled. "I've made a reputation for myself, Imogen. I'm obliged to have a poem to suit every occasion. And it pleases the mother to praise the child."

"He's a horrible little creature," Lady Imogen declared. "I will never forget what he did to me at Richmond. Really, Ingram, I do not see why you want to marry Phoebe, apart from her fortune. She hasn't a brain in her head and you must take that little beast in the bargain."

Lord Ingram looked at her critically. "I will admit that her fortune is a point in her favor, but you mustn't underestimate her very real charms, Imogen. But I don't suppose you understand things like that—generally you appreciate only the obvious. That is why I am somewhat at a loss to explain your attraction to Worthing."

"It is quite obvious," she snapped. "He has wealth, position and presence. As his wife I could become the foremost hostess in London. What more need there be?"

Lord Ingram sighed melodramatically. "I *had* hoped to find even a touch of the poet in you, sis. If only you had mentioned his scar, or perhaps his mysterious past."

"As to the scar, it is quite disfiguring, and I don't much care for mystery. But his fortune more than makes up for other shortcomings."

"Yes, we are all prepared to give up a great

139

deal for money—love, honor, even aesthetic sensibilities."

"As to that, we wouldn't have to give up a thing if Father weren't so tight with the purse strings, although you seem to be doing rather better in that regard lately. As for me, I am doing my best to advance your suit with the so-innocent Phoebe, I expect you to perform the same service for me as regards Worthing."

"While I sympathize entirely with your motives, sis, I would like to see you form a friendship just once for reasons other than financial gain."

"Do shut up, Ingram, you are the most horrible bore," she said, then noticing the approach of an admirer, she flashed a brilliant smile and came alive again.

Chapter Ten

By the time Justin Worthing had danced with all
four Anne Boleyns, including a second dance with
Lady Imogen, and had done his duty by several
wives of government ministers, he was heartily
bored with the whole proceeding. He wished
fervently that he could make his excuses and go
home, but as he was already home, that would be
impossible. He reached for his pocket watch, but
was frustrated yet again and so passed unobtrusively into the hallway to consult the clock
standing there.

It was only twenty minutes past eleven. Worthing had thought it much closer to midnight, at
which time would be the unmasking and then
supper. Followed, no doubt, he thought grimly, by
several more hours of dancing while he played the
genial host until the last guests left.

He was about to go back into the ballroom to

dutifully seek a partner for the next dance, when a voice from behind addressed him, "Your Majesty." As soon as he realized that this was directed at himself, he turned around to see a woman curtsying deeply before him.

He felt rather foolish and said gruffly, "No need to stand on ceremony—or kneel. You may rise."

The lady held out her hand and he took it to help her up. He examined her curiously, for he did not remember seeing her before, and although her face was half-obscured by the mask she wore, that part he could see told him that the whole was undoubtedly beautiful. Her neck was long and graceful, the skin revealed by her square-cut bodice smooth and milky white, her hair hung down her back in a riot of dark curls, lit here and there by flashes of auburn and even gold. In spite of himself, he smiled.

"Have we been introduced?" he asked, forcing his voice to coldness, for he remembered his words to Stone earlier of the dangers of a masked ball and was not unaware that this lady might even now have a doting mama eagerly watching their every move.

"Sire, I would have thought there was no need for an introduction," she said, her voice vaguely familiar so he was sure they *had* met before, although he could not remember where. "I am the Lady Jane Seymour." Her perfectly shaped mouth was curved in a delicate and slightly ironic smile and there was a glint of green from the two slits in her mask.

Worthing threw his head back and laughed. "At last, a lady with some originality. If I had seen

142

another false pearl or finger, I would have gone straight upstairs to bed."

"I am happy Your Majesty finds me pleasing," she said demurely. "I would be most honored if Your Majesty would ask me to dance."

"I am sure you would," Worthing said, still wary despite his immediate attraction to her.

The green eyes flashed him a knowing look. "I assure you, Your Majesty, I am laying no trap for you, I am entirely unattended. But perhaps you are wise to be cautious. Had I been true to my namesake, I should have waited for you to notice me."

Worthing appreciated her forthright approach and chose to believe she was speaking the truth, so he bowed graciously and said, "Let us then consider that all has gone according to history. I have now noticed you, Lady Jane, and I order you to dance with your monarch."

"Your wish is my command, sire," and she took his arm readily as he led her back into the ballroom.

There followed the most delightful dance Worthing had that evening, or possibly in his life. Perhaps one of the reasons he always disliked balls was that he was not the best dancer, and while a missed step or two usually went unnoticed in a country dance, he had more than once torn a flounce on a lady's hem during a waltz. But the Lady Jane Seymour seemed to float in his arms as lightly as a feather, adjusting herself easily to his every movement, so that he hardly concentrated on his feet at all, as was usually necessary, but for the first time was able to enjoy the feeling of gliding in time to the

music. Their conversation was easy and unforced
too, with not a single reference to the weather
Instead, his partner remarked that it would be a
wondrous thing indeed if everyone present were
suddenly transformed into the monarch they were
supposed to represent, and they spent some time
in cheerful conjecture until gradually even
conversation was unnecessary.

Their mutual pleasure was observed by Lady
Imogen whose dancing partner silently suffered
having his feet trodden upon as she tried to keep
an eye on them, a great fury mounting in her
breast. She did not know who the girl was, but
she knew whom she was dressed as, for Lady
Imogen had seen the portrait the costume was
modeled after. Silently, she cursed whatever evil
genius had prompted her to dress as Anne
Boleyn. If she had chosen to be Lady Jane
Seymour, she would have had only one com-
petitor, and that a poor one, for this Lady Jane's
costume was quite shabby, really, and nothing to
the one Lady Imogen would have had.

When the dance was over, Worthing was
reluctant to leave his partner and so suggested a
walk in the garden.

"Certainly," she said with a laugh in her voice
that once again prompted the sensation that he
had met her before. "But please remember, Your
Majesty, that it was entirely your suggestion and
do not again accuse me of being too forward."

"I never accused you of any such thing," he
protested as he led her out the door.

"Not in so many words," she admitted, "but
your tone spoke volumes."

In the garden, where the air was cool and

refreshing after the stuffiness of the ballroom, Worthing took her to a spot where they could be apart from the other strolling couples.

"Now perhaps you will tell me who you are," he demanded abruptly, after a brief silence.

"I have told you, sire, I am the Lady Jane Seymour," she replied gently.

"Yes, but won't you remove your mask for me?" He removed his own as he spoke, for the heat of the ballroom had caused him to perspire.

"When the time is right I will remove it."

"I feel very foolish—I am sure we have met before, yet I cannot place your voice."

"Perhaps we have met before in another lifetime," she suggested, deliberately mysterious.

He scowled slightly, "That is not what I meant."

"I see there is a limit to the amount of fantasy you will accept," she said with a light laugh. "How about this for an alternative—" She paused for a moment, forming the words in her mind before she spoke. "Perhaps I am an angel, sent to this earth to cure you of your aversion to beautiful women."

"I have no such aversion," he said, turning away abruptly.

"I am happy to hear you say that, but I do not quite believe you." She moved around so that he had to face her once more. "They told me up here," she cast her eyes skyward for a moment as a smile played on her lips, "that it had something to do with this." She ran her finger lightly across his scar, as she had been wanting to do for a long time.

He took her hand to move it away from his

face, but did not let it go. "Deuce take it, woman!" he exclaimed softly. "You would have done better to dress as Anne Boleyn, for I think you are a witch!"

"And bewitching?" she asked mischievously, but in the look he gave her was the light of dawning recognition, so she turned away quickly and said, "You need not speak of it if you do not care to. There is no reason for you to satisfy my idle curiosity. But I feel you have held it inside you for a long time and perhaps would feel better if you divulged the whole tale to a sympathetic listener, as I am."

He gazed down upon her and the moonlight and garden lights played through her hair so that she did indeed look like a haloed angel.

He smiled. "I feel somehow that you already know the story and do not need me to repeat it."

"I know something of it," she admitted. "I know that you were in love with a woman, a woman doubtless of great beauty, who somehow played you false."

"In love with her—no. Infatuated, most definitely, but I do not believe now that I was ever in love with her."

"Would it help you to speak of it, Justin?"

He started at her use of his Christian name, but was reassured by her gentle tone. "Yes," he said finally, "yes, I will tell you of it, if you really wish to hear, for it is a sordid little tale."

"Go on," she prompted, placing her hand over his.

He took her hand absently, and gazing beyond her, began haltingly, "There was a woman, as you say, of great beauty but small fortune and with

146

a father who prompted her to seek her best opportunity. I was mad about her, begging her repeatedly to marry me, but she always refused. You see, I was a younger son and there did not seem to be any hope of my ever coming into the title, for Richard had just been born and my brother had his heir. And of course there was Edward himself. I always felt myself to be but a poor copy of him. He was taller, better looking and always at ease with women, while I was rather shy and studious." He smiled slightly. "I never held it against him, you understand. For me it was a fact of life. But I did resent it a little when he continued to cut me out with every lady I was interested in, even after his marriage. It did seem a trifle unfair."

She squeezed his hand gently. "I should not have been cut out," she assured him.

He laughed slightly. "It is very kind of you to say so, but then you did not know Edward. He always knew the right things to say, the right compliments to make, whereas I was always tongue-tied and awkward, never any good at small talk or light pleasantries. I still am not," he added ruefully.

"I should not have been cut out," she repeated more firmly. "But you stray from your story."

"Of course. Well, there wasn't much to it, really. Poor Phoebe was still sickly after Richard's birth and Edward was feeling rather restless, I suppose. He ran off with this woman—the one I was mad about. I am sure he didn't mean to stay away permanently, but had plans to return with her to London and set her up comfortably, but of course he couldn't do this outright, her father

147

would never have permitted it. So they ran off, and I, in the rashness of my youth, ran after them. The only reason I caught up with them was that there had been an accident with the coach and I arrived to find my brother at death's door, for he had been thrown beneath the wheel and crushed."

"I am so sorry," she murmured.

"*She,* of course, had suffered no injury, but as we waited at the inn until Edward—until Edward could be moved, her father arrived. He awaited no explanations, but immediately assumed it was I who had compromised his daughter. We had a fight, in which I received this scar, and afterward I offered to restore her good name and all was made well. Excepting, of course, that Edward died from his injuries."

"But what happened afterward? I know you did not marry her."

"No, fortunately I was spared from that fate. What happened was simply that she took a great dislike to me, because of my disfigurement, and very shortly afterward ran off with an Italian count. I have not seen her or her father since, but I did vow that I would never trust a woman again, nor allow my head to be turned by mere beauty." He laughed shortly after he had said this, for even as he spoke them, the words of the promise he had made five years before sounded childish and petulant.

"And do you mean still to live by that promise?" she asked.

"I suppose I have," he said. "Perhaps not consciously, but I have certainly never been

interested in a woman since."

"What about Lady Imogen? I thought you wished to make her your wife."

"You do know a great deal about me, don't you?" he asked her, smiling. "Then you probably also know that Lady Imogen would be just the right sort of wife for me."

"It depends on what you mean by the right sort. But do you really think it wise to marry without affection?"

He looked down at her and suddenly knew the answer to that, and it was very different from what he might have said an hour ago. "And what is your interest in it?"

For the first time during their conversation she was nonplussed. "I don't know," she said, suddenly removing her hand from his. "I, too, have made a similar vow to myself, that I would never trust a man again, but now it seems very silly."

"Yes," he agreed, and they gazed for a long moment into each other's eyes.

The spell was broken by the sound of a bell ringing in the ballroom, indicating that it was midnight and time to unmask.

"Now I must see your face!" Worthing declared, and without waiting for her to unfasten it herself, he swiftly removed her mask.

"Are you any the wiser?" she asked, laughing.

He shook his head ruefully. He did not recognize her, but still there was the haunting familiarity, the feeling that he knew her from some other time and place. "I am almost ready to accept your explanation of having met you in another lifetime," he said, "but not quite."

"Perhaps not. Perhaps I am not an angel, either, but a fairy princess—in which case I must vanish immediately, for the clock has struck midnight and I might turn into something quite disagreeable right before your eyes." She took her mask back from him and made a motion as if to leave.

He stopped her, taking her by the wrist. "But you can't leave now—it's—don't you want to go into supper?" he finished lamely.

"Thank you, but I am not hungry," she replied, suddenly eager to be off.

"But when will we meet again? When can I see you?" He pulled her closer, reluctant to let her go without a promise of a future meeting.

"I cannot tell," she said. "Sometime, perhaps. Perhaps never."

"You are determined to remain mysterious, aren't you?"

"Yes," she replied. There was a sudden look of alarm in her eyes. "Please let me go—I can feel myself turning into a turnip." She forced some of her former lightness into these words.

He loosened his grip, and looked at her with dawning understanding. "Forgive me. I begin to see the reason for your childish vow and I should not wish to be the cause of its renewal. But as I have broken my vow tonight by placing my trust in you, I wish that you might be able to do the same for me."

Then she smiled, and the effect was so dazzling that he was once more struck by her beauty. "And so I shall," she said and without further warning threw her arms around his neck and kissed him.

While this was the very thing he had been wanting to do for the past few minutes, she nearly caught him unprepared, but he quickly recovered himself and returned her kiss, gently at first, then hungrily. Only an hour ago he would have declared that he would never again find pleasure in this activity, and was more than delighted to find himself proven wrong.

Then she broke away, as abruptly as she had come to him, and after one last, laughing glance, she ran lightly through the garden, back toward the house and was quickly lost to his sight.

He started after her, calling out futilely, "But we must meet again! I don't even know your name!" But he was checked in his pursuit when Lord Ingram Westham suddenly barreled into him from behind an arbor.

"Worthing!" he exclaimed, "come quickly! Phoebe's fainted and I can't seem to revive her." He led Worthing back behind the arbor, where Lady Fenworth lay spread out upon the grass, unconscious and extremely pale. Lord Ingram immediately knelt beside her and started rubbing her wrists, which occupation he had been pursuing before he had heard Worthing's voice and went to him for help.

"How did this happen?" Worthing asked gruffly, as he looked about aimlessly for some water to throw upon her face.

Despite his worried expression, Lord Ingram managed to look sheepish, too. "I was merely kissing her, Worthing—and I assure you she had no objection—when she simply fainted. Oh, God, I hope I haven't killed her."

"Don't flatter yourself, Westham," Worthing said, kneeling beside his sister-in-law. "Leave off that and help me loosen her gown and corset."

Lord Ingram had the grace to look embarrassed at this request, but he readily obliged. This, indeed, was just what Phoebe had needed and very shortly she was taking deep breaths as she opened her eyes with a flutter.

"What happened?" she asked weakly.

"It seems you were overcome—by something," Worthing said with a whimsical glance at Westham. He assisted her in rising.

"I *told* Dorcas this corset was far too tight," she said pettishly. Then as she looked at Lord Ingram she blushed deeply. "Oh, Ingram, I am so sorry."

"Not at all, my dear," he said, resuming his gallant air now that the danger had passed. "I should have been more careful of you—the heat has obviously taken its toll on you."

"Oh, dear!" she exclaimed, when she noticed that her gown no longer closed in the back. "However shall I return to the ball in this state?"

With a flourish, Lord Ingram removed his cloak and laid it across her shoulders. "Sir Walter is ever ready to serve his lady queen," he said elegantly.

Phoebe giggled uncertainly, still too much embarrassed to be at her ease.

"I suppose I can trust you to take my sister-in-law into supper without once again rendering her unconscious," Worthing said.

Lord Ingram decided that he was in too precarious a position to take offense at this remark, and so merely muttered, "Of course,

Worthing, what do you take me for?" as he took Phoebe's arm.

Worthing merely replied with a "Hmmm" that showed he had grave doubts on that score, and then with a brief nod left them to go into supper himself. He knew that by now there was no chance of catching up with the mysterious Lady Jane Seymour, but he did not know that her rapid exit had been noticed by two ladies of his acquaintance.

Christabel had to go through the ballroom to make her way upstairs again, and now without her mask. She did not see where Lady Imogen Westham stood chatting with Lady Larchmont, since she was not wearing her spectacles, but Lady Imogen noticed her and remarked to her companion,

"There is that woman who was dancing with Mr. Worthing a while ago. Who *can* she be?"

Lady Larchmont raised her lorgnette to look at the retreating figure. "It looks remarkably like— no, I am convinced it *is,* Miss Devlin!"

"Miss Devlin?" Lady Imogen inquired.

"She was our governess for a time," was the reply, and Lady Larchmont gave a brief description of the events leading up to Miss Devlin's dismissal, naturally attaching all blame to the governess, and ending with, "The daughter of an actor, too, a most unsuitable creature. I can't think why I hired her in the first place. And I certainly can't think how she came to be invited *here.*"

Lady Imogen was very interested in this news, for she recognized the name of Devlin and knew it was one that had been bothering her father of

153

late. So that is our little Irish cousin, she said to herself, very interesting, very interesting indeed.

Just then she noticed Worthing's return to the ballroom and went to remind him that he had promised to take her in to supper.

Chapter Eleven

That night, after the last of the guests finally bid him farewell, Justin Worthing went to bed still angry with himself that he had let the mysterious Lady Jane slip away without discovering her real name or how he might arrange to see her again. The memory of the laughing green eyes and the vibrant brown hair was so strong within him that Lady Imogen Westham found him to be a most unsatisfactory companion at supper, and even when he asked her to dance with him yet a third time, her triumph was hollow; for all the attention he paid her he might as easily have been dancing with a stick of wood.

In the cold, clear light of morning, however, the voice of reason within Worthing told him he was behaving like a fool and it was better he should never see this Lady Jane again. His ears burned when he recalled how much he had betrayed to her in confidence, prompted by nothing more than the magic of the moment and the general feeling of recklessness that invariably accompanies a masked ball. No, better that the lady should remain mysterious so that he need not be reminded how he had shared his most private thoughts with a total stranger.

But even so, emotions he had nearly forgotten he was capable of argued against his reason, so by the time he was dressed and ready to begin work for the day he was firm in his resolution to at least consult the guest list from the ball to determine Lady Jane's true identity and perhaps even ask others who were present if they had recognized her.

And so, after a brief greeting and disinterested inquiry into how she had slept, his first question to Miss Stone that morning was,

"I don't suppose you noticed the woman last night who was dressed as Lady Jane Seymour?" He deliberately tried to make this sound as casual as possible but felt he had failed miserably when Stone started abruptly and treated him to a piercing stare.

Christabel herself had been battling with what her answer would be should this question be posed, and now the words came out almost involuntarily. "No, I don't believe so," she said carefully, pushing her spectacles up with one finger. "I noticed a great many Anne Boleyns, but no Lady Jane."

"Deuce take it," Worthing muttered. "Would you be so kind as to ask Lady Fenworth when next you see her?"

"Certainly," Christabel said agreeably. "Mean

while, would you care to take a look at the guest list? Perhaps you can discover something from that." She offered this suggestion secure in the knowledge that he would discover nothing.

"Dammit, Stone," he said mildly, "I wish you would at least allow me the formality of making a request before you carry it out."

"But that would ruin my reputation for second-guessing you," she said with a laugh, and went into her own cubbyhole to fetch the list for him. Something in the way she laughed and the set of her head as she walked away from him caused Worthing to gaze after her with an acute feeling of déjà vu, but he quickly shook it off, telling himself that of course he had seen Stone walk into her office dozens of times and it was no good for him to be mooning about like any schoolboy in the first throes of puppy love, seeing a reflection of his beloved in everyone he met. He would follow the thing through in his usual efficient manner and if nothing came of it, he would simply forget about the elusive Lady Jane. Chances were she was probably a woman most unsuited to him or she would have behaved in a more openhanded, proper manner.

When Christabel brought the list, he glanced over it quickly, but all the names on it were familiar to him, except for a few young ladies, two of whom, Christabel readily explained, had been dressed as Anne Boleyn and one as Mary, Queen of Scots.

"So that was who I danced with," was all Worthing had to say as he handed the list back to Christabel. Then he squared his shoulders and assumed a more businesslike attitude, ready to begin work for the day.

"Would you like to see that piece of paper I was hiding from you last night?" Christabel asked him.

"What? Oh, yes—I had completely forgotten."

She returned with it quickly, as well as with a sheaf of papers which included the several dispatches containing information about the lost ships. She spread them out on Worthing's desk and then, retaining the same paper she had been working on the night before, she began to explain, choosing her words carefully.

"As you know, I have an acquaintance with Alexis Nichols, the second wife of my—cousin, Stephen Devlin—" For a moment she had nearly forgotten the relationship she claimed with her father. "Occasionally, I pay a call on her, as I did several days before the ball."

"That is very thoughtful of you, I am sure, but what has it to do with this other business?" Worthing asked impatiently.

"I am coming to that," she replied, exactly as she was used to speak to Richard. "Now all this is the purest conjecture, you understand, but something Alexis said about the manager of the Majestic Theatre made me think that he might be our man. He is Spanish—"

"Stone, if we were to question every Spaniard in England on suspicion, we would have lost the war before we were finished," Worthing interrupted testily.

"Do let me finish," Christabel said with a flash of temper. "Do you think I am so stupid that I don't realize that?"

Worthing generously acknowledged that perhaps she was not and that she needn't fly into the boughs about it.

She gave a little sniff and continued. "She was complaining about his frequent absences from the theater when he was needed during a performance, especially one time when he missed an opening night. Now, I have checked the dates of when this manager was absent from his theater and they correspond remarkably well with the dates information may have been passed on to the enemy." She handed the slip of paper to Worthing and he took it and studied it carefully, his brow creasing.

"All these dates are mere approximations," he said.

"I prefer to consider them educated guesses."

"That is all very well, but how do we know this Spaniard of yours was not simply visiting his mistress?"

"And why should his mistress live outside of London?" Christabel countered with a twinkle.

Worthing merely grunted. "And what is this column—'Am. Perf.'?"

"Frequently—every second Monday, it seems—Santanos allows the theater to be let by some nobleman or other for a performance of amateur theatricals—audience by invitation only. The interesting thing is that his absences always come immediately after one of these amateur events. Do you see here?" She leaned over his shoulder to point to the paper. "We filed the requisition sheets for *The Prosperity* on the twentieth of April. She set sail for Cadiz on the Sunday. On Monday, the twenty-third, an amateur performance was held at the Majestic. In the next few days Santanos was absent and on the second of May we learned that *The Prosperity* had been taken. The fate of *The Wayward Lady* follows the same pattern."

"And you believe that the information was passed to Santanos during these amateur performances."

Christabel nodded. "It is a perfect cover—whoever it is does not make himself conspicuous by visiting the theater alone, but waits until there are a number of other gentlemen around, so he is lost in the crowd."

"By God, you may have something here, Stone," Worthing said excitedly. "But I notice you have put *The Endeavor* on the list as well, although we have heard nothing about her."

"Nothing yet," Christabel said gravely.

Worthing set his mouth in a tight line. "We must do something about this. *The Fame* is being outfitted now and is due to set sail in two days. We cannot risk losing another ship."

"We have not yet filed her route. We must use the false report we have ready and see if it will lead us to the traitor."

"Then I suppose we will have to attend one of these performances ourselves."

"Yes," Christabel agreed. "It will probably be held on Monday."

Worthing groaned. "That is all I need, to have to sit for hours listening to Monk Lewis recite his doggerel. The prospect is uninviting."

Christabel grinned. "You will be doing it for king and country."

"I hope I will be doing it for something, for I do not wish to waste an evening of my life following a false trail. We still have nothing more to go on than a series of coincidences, accompanied by pure speculation. But perhaps when I talk it over with Duxton he will be able to shed some new light on the matter. At least to gain his support for—"

"No!" Christabel objected suddenly.

Worthing looked at her with surprise. "No, what? You do not think he will shed any new light?"

"I do not think you should tell him anything," she said. "I—I should have told you this at the first, for it was what led me to discover the rest." She took a deep breath. "When I was last at the theater I heard the duke of Duxton promise a sum of money to Santanos."

Worthing sat in stunned silence for a moment, but when he finally replied his tone was calm and considered. "You are certain of this? You do not think you might be mistaken?"

"I heard their conversation from around the corner, during which the duke quite plainly promised one thousand pounds on account."

"Ah—you only heard this. Perhaps it was someone who only sounded like the duke."

"I looked around the corner. It was indeed the duke."

"I see." Worthing was thoughtful again. "I cannot believe it," he said finally. "Duxton has never been connected with anything underhanded. I cannot imagine that he would be involved in anything of this sort. Are you quite sure the man he spoke to was Santanos? Could he not have been giving the money for some other purpose?"

"What other purpose?" Christabel asked. "He is not known for his charity."

Worthing gave an uneasy laugh. "Quite true." He piled up all the papers Christabel had placed in front of him, making a nice, neat stack. "But all of this is still merest conjecture. I will not speak to Duxton of it, but until we have something more to go on I will make no accusations, either. We will attend this amateur performance on Monday night and see what we can discover there."

Christabel nodded. Then, thinking it best to change the subject now, she glanced quickly at her diary and said, "I almost forgot to remind you—a woman is coming this morning to be interviewed for the position of governess."

"Good God!" Worthing exclaimed. "Haven't enough to worry about? I never know what to say to these women."

"Yes, I know," Christabel acknowledged with a twinkle. "It does make you so uncomfortable."

Worthing laughed. "Why don't you do it for me? You know more about it than I do—you've been a governess. Offer her twenty-five a year—thirty if she seems worth it—and don't let me be bothered about it."

Lady Imogen and Lord Ingram Westham were early afternoon callers on Lady Fenworth that day. While others had been to call that morning, too, they had been content to leave their cards, for Lady Fenworth was a trifle indisposed after the exertions of the previous evening, but upon their announcement, Lady Imogen and Lord Westham were most generously invited to wait upon her in her boudoir.

Lord Westham took this as a hopeful sign, for he had feared that he might have damaged his suit by his too eager behavior at the ball—he was not used to females fainting from his kisses, even if the corset and not the kisses were to blame. He had confessed this fear to his sister on the way home the night before and she turned on him roundly, saying, "I shouldn't be at all surprised, Ingram, if Phoebe had nothing more to do with you. More heavy-handed behavior I never heard of, and certainly never expected from *you.*" Of course, she was somewhat sharper than she had meant to be, for her own suit with Worthing was not prospering either. Despite her best efforts and most obvious hints, she had been unable to get him alone and while they had danced three times, no one but she had made any veiled remarks that there might be something serious behind his attentions. So she agreed to accompany Ingram on his visit, both to help him patch things up with Lady Fenworth and in hopes that she might again see Mr. Worthing.

They found Phoebe arranged artistically upon a divan, looking a trifle pale but pleased to see them nonetheless.

"My dear Phoebe!" Lady Imogen exclaimed upon seeing her, "what a splendid ball it was. Everyone has agreed it was a great success. Did you not think so, Ingram?"

"An evening to warm the heart, a lifetime of pleasure and delight squeezed into a mere four or five hours," Lord Ingram declared with a flourish as he seated himself in answer to Phoebe's unspoken invitation.

Phoebe colored prettily at this praise. "Would you care for some refreshment?" she asked. She

carefully avoided Lord Ingram's eye, preferring not
to remember the rather grueling experience she
had suffered at his hands the night before, and
hoping that he would not notice any difference in
her attitude. She was beginning to think that
perhaps she should not have invited them upstairs
after all, but she had been bored after her morning
of solitude.

Lord Ingram did notice the slight coolness in her
demeanor toward him, and with a helpless glance
at Lady Imogen, he launched into new raptures
about Lady Fenworth's attire at the ball, the wonderful refreshments served there, the excellence of
the music, all to no avail, for Phoebe replied
merely with an absent smile—she never could
follow him when he spoke in this manner. At last
Lady Imogen gave her brother a quelling glance
which shut him up, and she made some thoughtful
inquiries into the health of the young earl, which
thankfully brought Phoebe out of herself and
cheered her up considerably. Dorcas brought a
tray of tea and cakes and they were soon all cozily
chatting about the ball, remembering each person's costume and laughing at the more outlandish
ones.

They were interrupted by the unexpected but
most welcome arrival of Worthing. Greetings were
exchanged all around, and Lady Imogen pretended
to blush gracefully as she extended her hand to
him, for she was certain that this uncharacteristic
behavior of his was an indication that her recent
doubts were completely unfounded and that his
interest in her was as strong as it had ever been

"I can't stop with you long," he said amiably
"Stone is waiting below to finish some dictation

and we have a meeting this afternoon. However, when I heard you were visiting I thought I might join you just for a while."

"Mr. Worthing, how kind of you," Lady Imogen said, her dark eyes flashing. "Your presence was all that was needed to make this afternoon quite perfect."

"Yes, of course," Worthing said gruffly, somewhat embarrassed by this remark.

"At least stay and have some tea with us," Lady Fenworth requested. "Then we can pretend you have come to call just like a real person."

This artless remark won a smile from him as he admitted the novelty of pretending to be a real person. He pulled up a chair next to Lady Imogen, and Phoebe sent Dorcas for another cup.

"All London is buzzing about the great success of your ball," Lady Imogen said, "you are to be congratulated."

"I?" Worthing asked with a puzzled expression. "I had nothing at all to do with either the success or failure of the thing. I understand you had a greater part in the planning than I."

Lady Imogen acknowledged this modestly.

"And, of course, Stone made all the arrangements," he added, and then with a laugh, "We nearly submitted a list of refreshments to the government and ordered a supply of arms for the ball."

Lady Imogen's laughter was forced after the mention of Miss Stone.

"Imagine our poor lads on the Peninsula trying to load their guns with cream puffs," Lord Ingram said.

"Yes," Worthing replied shortly as he imagined

this too vividly for his own comfort.

Dorcas returned with the extra cup and when Worthing had been provided with tea he turned to Lady Imogen and said, "But I really joined you here because I hoped you might shed some light on a little mystery for me."

"Mr. Worthing, I am always eager to be of service to you," Lady Imogen said with a sly smile. "Pray, how can I help?"

He gave her a quick, critical glance, noticing perhaps for the first time, her too obvious effort to please him. But this look quickly vanished and was replaced by a friendly, noncommittal smile as he said, "There was someone present at the ball last night—a young lady—and I was wondering if you might be able to tell me who she was."

Lady Imogen's brows came together in a swift unattractive scowl, but her smile was once again charming as she said, "But how very mysterious! I should be glad to oblige you if you will describe her to me."

"She was dressed as Lady Jane Seymour," Worthing explained, "and had a great quantity of long dark hair."

Lady Imogen's smile was now triumphant as she recognized in this description the young lady she and Lady Larchmont had seen leaving the ball with such undue haste. "It so happens I can help you," she said, "and I can certainly understand why you wish to learn her identity. I am sure she cannot have been invited to the ball, but must have pushed her way in somehow."

This was unwelcome news to Worthing. "Indeed?" he said.

Lady Imogen nodded primly. "Yes, it seems she

a certain Miss Devlin. She once was governess o Lady Larchmont's two children but was discovered to be a little *fast*, shall we say, and Lady Larchmont was forced to dismiss her."

"I see," he said, frowning.

"Yes, I noticed that you danced with her," Lady Imogen said, with an attempt at nonchalance, "such an *obvious* young woman, I am surprised you asked her to stand up."

"As it happens, she asked me," Worthing admitted reluctantly.

"Well, there you have it! Not at all a *proper* young woman."

Lord Ingram, who had been engaged in his own, one-sided conversation with Lady Fenworth, heard this last remark. "Who is not a proper young woman?" he asked with interest.

"Just someone who was at the ball last night," Lady Imogen answered casually. "She was dressed as Lady Jane Seymour and seems to have pushed her way in."

"How is it I did not notice her?" Lord Ingram asked. "I am always on the lookout for improper young women." He gave Worthing a conspiratorial wink.

Worthing returned with a withering glance. "I believe you were otherwise occupied, Westham." For once Phoebe took a meaning readily and wished that somehow she might disappear from the room and never have to face Lord Ingram again.

After a few more minutes of unbearable chatter in which he took little part, Worthing stood up. "Thank you for your help, Lady Imogen. As you say, this Lady Jane sounds to me a most improper

167

sort of person—it is as well that she left the bal
early." He took his leave of the company to returr
to his work.

He was still so preoccupied as he returned to the
library that he barely noticed the woman Christ
abel introduced as Miss Jones.

"Mr. Worthing," she said, more loudly, "I am
taking Miss Jones upstairs to meet Richard now
unless you would like to have a word with he
first."

His attention was finally forced to rest upon thi
nondescript female. She appeared to be abou
forty years of age, dressed plainly in brown, he
mousy hair pulled neatly back and with protrud
ing, watery blue eyes regarded him nervously.

"Miss Jones," he said, "I am very pleased to
meet you. I suppose Miss Stone has asked all the
particulars?"

"Yes, sir," she answered, "and I would be very
pleased to come and work for you." Her voice wa
high-pitched, but not unpleasant.

"Very good," Worthing said, with a wave o
dismissal. Then, almost as they were out of th
door he stopped them, saying, "Stone, this cousir
of yours—Devlin?"

"Yes?" Christabel asked, turning around.

"You wouldn't happen to know if he had an
young female relations—a niece or perhaps a
daughter?"

Fortunately, Christabel's disguising cream hid
the sudden loss of color in her face. "Why do you
ask?"

"It seems someone saw this Lady Jane at th
ball and recognized her as a certain Miss Devlin.
thought there might be some connection."

"I don't believe so," Christabel said firmly, having regained her composure swiftly. "It is a fairly common name."

"I suppose so," he said indistinctly. He noticed again the other woman standing uncertainly in the doorway and said, "Pleasure to meet you, Miss Jones," then he seated himself behind his desk.

Chapter Twelve

"Christabel, what game are you playing?"

Christabel avoided her stepmother's eyes "Whatever do you mean, Alex? Why should I be playing at anything?"

Alexis looked at her shrewdly and indicated the costume Christabel had come to return. "I can understand why you would want to put on fancy dress and make a splash at the ball as the mysterious Lady Incognita. But from what you have told me, it seems you have done it solely for the benefit of your Mr. Worthing."

"Don't be so silly, Alex," she said crossly. "I did it for my own pleasure and to show up my cousin."

"Just what I have said—to show her up to Justin Worthing. And do you think he made the comparison to your advantage?"

"I have no idea, to be sure," Christabel said with a hint of sulkiness. "And if he has, why then it only proves what I have maintained all along—that all men are interested only in a woman's beauty and care nothing for the person inside. Mr. Worthing is no different from any other man in that respect, else why should he prefer me dressed as a beautiful Lady Jane and not as the dowdy Miss Stone?"

"Ah! So that is what is troubling you. Your little plan worked rather too well and now you are disappointed to find that Justin Worthing, whom you so admire, is no different from any other man."

"I am not disappointed, I am delighted to find my thesis proven correct once more."

"Please don't jump on your bandbox for *me,*" Alexis said, laughing. "No one would be more pleased than I to learn you had fallen in love with Worthing."

"I have done no such thing," Christabel said with something less than conviction. "You know I shall never fall in love with any man who loves me only for my appearance. I am many other things besides beautiful."

"Such as stubborn and short-tempered?" Alexis suggested. "I hardly believe a man would find those qualities attractive."

"Deuce take it!" Christabel cried, pacing about. "If I had known you were going to read me a lecture on my shortcomings, I should have simply dropped the costume off and been on my way."

"I suppose that is one of your employer's expressions you have picked up?" was the mild return.

"What is?" Christabel asked pettishly.

"I hardly like to say it myself," Alexis said, "but believe the words you used were 'deuce take it.' "

Suddenly Christabel's sense of humor got the better of her and she laughed. "I am sorry, Alex, I will try to control my tongue, but I am afraid I have been too much in Worthing's company lately."

"Yes," Alexis agreed pointedly, then noticing Christabel's expression hastily added, "Please do not fly off the handle again, my dear, I have enough of that sort of thing from that wretched little Spaniard."

This reference reminded Christabel of the other thing that had been on her mind, and she asked cautiously, not wishing to appear too interested and thus arouse Alexis's suspicions, "Has he been giving you trouble again?"

"I think he has forgotten he is running a professional theater," Alexis said, a hint of her own temper showing. "I have just learned that we are only to have four performances of *The Country Wife* next week because he is hiring out the hall on Wednesday for another of his amateur nights. Generally, he does it only on Mondays, when the theater is unoccupied anyway, but to cancel a regular performance—it is unspeakable!"

Christabel murmured sympathetically, even while she carefully catalogued this information in her mind. "Have you been able to advance my suit with the duke at all?" she asked finally, apparently changing the subject.

Was it her imagination or did Alexis deliberately avoid her gaze?

"I am sorry, my dear, but I have not seen the duke for some time. Things stand as they were."

"Oh," Christabel was surprised by this reply "But I saw him at the theater the other night, thought surely he was there to see you."

Alexis bowed her head. "I suppose you might have." She paused a moment, then went on with deliberation. "I might as well tell you, then. I have been seeing the duke quite frequently for late suppers after my performances. For some reason he has taken an interest in me."

"Alex!" Despite her familiarity with the ways of the theater and actresses, Christabel was shocked.

"Now, there is no need to take that tone with me, young lady," Alexis said severely. "While I have not—yielded—to the duke, I did not want to turn him away completely for hopes of a chance to advance your cause with him. Besides I find him an agreeable companion," she finished, as though that were justification for anything.

"But, Alex!" Christabel cried. "How can you find him an agreeable companion after the way he has treated me?"

"So far he has not treated you any way at all, but has been most diligent in ignoring you. I am merely attempting to transfer an interest in me to one in you. I do try to speak of you often and I believe I am making progress. And who knows—" She shrugged. "If something comes of it for me in the end, well, I am not getting any younger."

Christabel was more upset by this last statement than Alexis knew. She did not care for the duke at all and suddenly saw how he might be using Alexis—whom she did care for very much.

"Has it not occurred to you," Christabel asked finally, "that the duke might be interested in coming to the theater for other reasons than to see you?" She knew, even as she said it, that this was ungracious, but to her surprise Alexis laughed.

"My dear, I am not that taken in by my own charms," she said easily. "Of course, by coming to the theater the duke has put himself in a better position to keep an eye on his own son, who has taken up with one of our girls. A rackety fellow your cousin, and his father is very naturally concerned that he will make a fool of himself. Not an unlikely possibility where Maisie is concerned, for she always has an eye open for a good chance."

Christabel digested this information carefully but saw nothing in it to change her mind about the duke or his intentions. That his son also had a kind of connection with the Majestic was of interest only insofar as it afforded him another reason for visiting there and another cover for his true purposes. But despite her now unshakable conviction of Duxton's guilt, she was still unable to convince Worthing of it. But his stubbornness on this point was not the only thing that made her more than usually short-tempered with him. Alexis had reminded her that she was not pleased with the outcome of her little masquerade at the ball. She had been pleased at the time; so pleased that she had laid awake most of that night remembering over and over the joy of his kisses and the wonderful feeling of his arms about her, the way he had opened to her so readily and placed his trust in her. But further reflection in the days following had brought her to the conclusions she had voiced to Alexis—that he had never done for Miss Stone, whom he was on terms of friendship with, as he had done for a beautiful stranger who had nothing more to recommend herself to his confidence than her beauty. In a way she felt it to be a denial of herself, all the more painful coming from one, despite all her protests to the contrary, with whom she was in love.

When she reported to Worthing with what she had learned from Alexis, there began again another argument about Duxton's culpability, or perhaps it was merely a continuation of the same argument.

"I cannot believe it of him," Worthing repeated firmly. "He hates Bonaparte and all the French—he has said as much a thousand times. I cannot believe he would sell us out to them."

"But you cannot deny the possibility," Christabel told him once more. "And even though we have nothing more than suspicions at this point, we must act on them in some way and thus gain more proof."

"I agree with you, and that is why I have decided to ask him about it, straight out," he said at last. "It is the only decent thing to do."

"Ask him!" Christabel exclaimed. "That would be a very stupid thing to do! To ask him would be to alert him that we are on his trail and then we would never be able to catch him."

"Exactly," Worthing agreed. "And if he is guilty, it will give him the chance to disappear gracefully, without a scandal."

"And then we shall never be able to catch Santanos, either."

"There is no reason for you to raise your voice with me, Miss Stone, my hearing is everything it should be."

"But it seems your reason is not!" Christabel retorted and was very close to bursting into tears, until she observed the stubborn set of Worthing's jaw and the marked resemblance he bore to his nephew when he wished to have his way. And so instead she laughed, and Worthing, uncertain, joined in with her, tentatively at first then, seeing the point, more heartily, and they both laughed until they were nearly out of breath.

"It is ridiculous for us to argue so," Christabel said finally. "We are both on the same side. Can we not reach a compromise?"

"What do you suggest?" Worthing asked amiably.

"Is there not some way you could speak to the duke, feel him out, without revealing your suspicions?"

"I suppose—" he hesitated.

"Come, come, Mr. Worthing, you are an intelligent man, surely you can think of something."

"I am glad to see you have changed your tactics, Stone. A little more flattery and a little less henpecking will not come amiss." And they both laughed again.

"And now, as to Wednesday night," Christabel said, quelling her laughter. "I have been thinking that it might be best if we conceal ourselves somewhere around the theater instead of going there openly. I know the theater well and have thought of the very place. Then we can keep a close eye on the duke and we will be two witnesses to his treachery!"

"Conceal ourselves? Why must we conceal ourselves? This is sounding more havey-cavey by the minute."

"Yours is not a familiar face there. If the duke sees you, he may catch on. And, of course, I shouldn't be allowed in at all." She gave a slight grin. "The subject matter is often unfit for ladies' ears."

"It is often unfit for anyone's ears," Worthing agreed. "Then why don't I go by myself? We are still not certain that we will discover anything and there is no reason for both of us to waste an evening."

Christabel's face fell. "Oh, if you would rather do it alone—"

"No, no!" he assured her. "It was foolish of me to suggest it, of course. I cannot do it alone. I only thought you might find it boring."

"Boring?" Christabel protested. "I think it will be fun!"

He smiled wryly. "You are doing your best to make it so, what with secret hiding places and the like. Will we need disguises as well?" He shook his head. "If only Rodgers had not come down with consumption."

"What do you mean by that?" she flashed.

"I mean that I should have been involved in none of this, for Rodgers had a singular lack of imagination."

"And I suppose between the two of you, you should have been content to lose ship after ship, until the war was lost."

"I do not doubt that eventually we should have caught the traitor," Worthing said, then noticing a slight pout appear on her face, hastily added, "but then I should have missed all this *fun!*"

Her smile returned and he noticed, not for the first time, a peculiar warmth he felt when she looked at him in that way. Coming down with something, he told himself, and turned away from her slightly.

But while he was now content to go along with Christabel's plans, privately he thought they would come to nothing. While the evidence of the dates was quite convincing, the whole thing was still a long shot. And while he fervently hoped that Christabel's suspicions of the duke would come to nothing, too, these suspicions continued to plague him and he looked for an opportunity to speak to Duxton, feel him out, as Stone had put it. He was even more anxious for such an interview when the next day they received news that the *Endeavor* had been taken, fortunately not destroyed as the first two ships had been, for she carried gold to pay the troops and that was too rare and valuable a commodity for even the French to send to the bottom of the sea.

No one seemed more upset by this most recent loss than the duke of Duxton himself. He stormed up and down the chambers of the War Office, even going so far as to tell Lord Liverpool exactly what he thought about the efficiency of the ministry which wasn't much, and declaring loudly to all who would listen that while he was against it before, he would now wholeheartedly support a regency if he thought the prince would be able to put *real* men in the government.

To Worthing these did not sound like the words of a traitor, and he expressed his own anger at the loss of the *Endeavor* by having another argument with Stone on that point. And perhaps he might have been convinced to abandon the whole idea of Duxton's guilt if Stone had once more argued against him. But this time she agreed with every thing he said, that Duxton could not possibly be guilty and that there was probably no connection at all between the loss of three ships at sea and activities at the Majestic Theatre. In the face of such complete support, he could do nothing but go on with their original plan.

The next day, when Duxton's initial anger had abated somewhat, Worthing found the moment he had been seeking to speak with him. As he was passing the door that led to the duke's chambers, he noticed him sitting quite quietly behind his desk, busy with some papers.

Worthing rapped lightly on the door frame and was welcomed in.

"Worthing, I was just going over this agreement for exchange of prisoners—perhaps you can advise me."

They spoke about it for a few minutes until Worthing was able to introduce his own topic of conversation. He asked, with as much indifference as he could muster, "Tell me, Duxton, what do you know of the performances at the Majestic Theatre?" He winced even as he said it, for he knew it sounded bald and ham-fisted.

"What do you mean?" the duke answered with some surprise.

Worthing attempted to tone down his apparent interest. "It is just that my sister-in-law has asked me to take her there some evening. She has heard they have a very good company. I was wondering if you knew anything of it—I don't keep up with these things myself." He was satisfied with that speech, it had a sufficient injection of indifference to—he hoped—throw off the duke's suspicions.

"I am not certain I've ever been to the Majestic Theatre myself," the duke said shortly. Then mistaking Worthing's look of surprise as an objection to his rudeness, he added, "One theater is much like another, you know, unless there is a certain actress you've a fancy for." He broke off suddenly and became very interested in straightening out the papers on his desk. "You should ask my son, you know, he is more informed on that sort of thing. He has taken up with an actress recently, I believe."

"I will ask him, then."

"Yes, do. Of course, if Lady Fenworth wishes to go there, I should be happy to take her. Perhaps we could make up a party some evening this week. Not Wednesday, for I am already engaged, but any other night."

"I will tell her that you mentioned it," Worthing said.

"Splendid!" the duke said, a little too heartily. "I was quite taken with Lady Fenworth, you know. I might admit that I've an inclination to cut out my own son with her. You've no objection to that, have you, Worthing?"

"No, no, certainly not," Worthing said absently, for he did not really hear this last remark. He was thinking about the implications of the duke's denial of any knowledge about the Majestic Theatre. Surely an innocent man would admit to being a frequent visitor there. "I am sure Phoebe would be happy to go to the theater with you," he said by way of dismissal. "She often complains that things are too slow this time of year."

"Oh?" The duke was surprised. "She seemed to me a woman particularly easy to please, but if the height of the Season is too slow for her, what must she do the rest of the year?"

Worthing realized what he had said and tried to

180

make amends, laughing nervously. "Well, you know women—they must always complain of something."

The duke frowned. "Really? Lady Fenworth did not strike me as a complaining sort of woman."

"No," Worthing agreed, "and indeed she is not. A more even, gentle disposition you could not hope to find."

"Yes, of course," the duke said, giving him a strange look. "Do take care of yourself, Worthing— I know the heat at this time of year frequently affects people very strongly."

"The heat? Oh, yes, the heat. We've been having some lovely weather lately." And with that he left the duke staring after him perplexedly.

After that interview, Worthing had no hesitations about going ahead with Christabel's plan, although he could still not see what good would come of it. It was not that he objected to the principle of the thing—if Duxton were a traitor, then he must be apprehended at all costs. What he objected to was the manner of the plan; he did not approve of skulking about and hiding behind draperies. But Stone seemed to have her heart set on this idea, and if she wanted to squeeze some amusement out of finding a traitor who had already sent a hundred or so men to imprisonment by the French and thousands of pounds worth of cargo to the bottom of the sea, then she was welcome to and he told her as much.

But when he said this to her, she did not lash out with a deprecating remark, as he had almost expected. Instead, she placed her hand on his arm and looked into his eyes, her gaze steady behind her spectacles.

181

"Do you think I have not laid awake at night thinking about that?" she asked him. "I assure you, I have felt it strongly. But the only alternative is inaction. Even if this seems like nothing more than a lark, at least we are *doing* something. And there is always the possibility that some good will come of it."

It was then that Duxton's last remark struck him as having some truth behind it—perhaps he *was* affected by the heat. For at that moment, he felt like nothing so much as reaching down to kiss Stone upon the lips. It was not because he felt some overwhelming desire for her, but simply because it seemed that it was exactly the right thing to do. But he hesitated too long; Stone withdrew from him to return to her work and the moment passed.

Then he knew he must be coming down with something, for even while the memory of the mysterious Lady Jane's kisses was still sweet on his lips, he had actually been considering kissing Stone, of all people. He was either coming down with something or going mad. Or perhaps he was just coming to his senses.

Chapter Thirteen

They sat waiting in Alexis Nichols's dressing room until the few workmen washing floors and sweeping out seats left so they could make their way unnoticed to their proposed hiding place on the second balcony. There was still almost an hour before the amateur performance was to begin, so Christabel was confident that they would have plenty of time to position themselves in the best spot for watching the proceedings of the evening.

As they waited they conversed in low voices, occasionally quiet as they listened for sounds in the corridor outside. But even as they spoke once more about what action they planned to take should they uncover some concrete evidence that night, Worthing was thinking very hard about something else, a decision he had made two days ago, and how best he might introduce the subject of that decision to the woman who now sat before him, regarding him calmly in the light of the single candle. What he finally did say aloud, though—that their presence here was a mistake and they would likely discover nothing—bore no relation at all to what was really on his mind.

Christabel smiled at him. "Let us not go through that litany again, please," she said. "We are here and we must make the most of our situation."

"To be sure we are here," Worthing agreed, "the question still is whether there is a situation that can be made the most of."

"But of course there is! For instance, what do you suppose Lady Imogen would make of this setting? I can easily guess what she would be thinking were she here in my place." Christabel batted her eyelashes in imitation of Lady Imogen. "Here I sit, in near darkness, completely alone with a handsome man, who is, by the by, also possessed of a large fortune and a bright future. No one knows where we are, let me see how easy it will be for me to wrap him around my little finger."

Worthing laughed. "And then she would doubtless force me into a compromising position, at which time her brother would burst through the door demanding I make an honest woman of her."

"Exactly! All your worst fears come true."

"I see several flaws in that scenario. First of all I am sure Lady Imogen does not think me handsome, and secondly I am not one to be taken in by a pair of fluttering eyelashes."

"That is too bad, for I have been practicing ever so hard to do it right," she said. "But I will make a third objection—Lady Imogen is so sure of you she would not feel the need for such trickery."

"Is she, by God? She should not be."

Christabel pushed her spectacles up with one finger. "She would make you the right sort of wife."

Worthing smiled wryly. "Yes, so I've often thought. But I have recently changed my mind about the right sort of wife for me."

Unaccountably, Christabel was suddenly aware that her heart was thumping quite loudly. She turned away from him slightly. "Don't tell me you have fallen in love with someone else."

"Fallen in love? No, I don't believe so. I am not even sure what that means any more."

A small sigh escaped from Christabel's lips, and she turned back to him with a wry smile. "I am so glad to hear it. For to fall in love I think you would have to break your long-standing vow and once more place your trust in a woman."

She was alarmed by his sudden scowl. "What do you know of any vow I might have made?"

"Why, nothing. Only what you have told me."

"What did I tell you?" He was perplexed.

It was lucky he could not see her face flush beneath the yellowish cream as she suddenly remembered when he had told her that. "Perhaps you did not tell me, then," she said lightly, "perhaps I merely deduced it."

"You are fond of deduction, are you not? That is what has brought us here." He broke off as they heard the rattlings of one of the workmen walking through the hallway outside. When he spoke again it was after a long pause, during which he had done much thinking. "Perhaps I might have fallen in love with Lady Imogen," he said reflectively, "but I should never have *liked* her, we have too little in common. In some ways I believe liking is much more important than loving."

"But real love only grows from liking," Christabel said, adjusting herself to this new train of thought.

"Do you think so? I don't know. One could conceivably fall in love and grow to like afterward. And one can like without loving."

"You are growing too philosophical now," Christabel admonished. She was suddenly anxious to abandon this subject, even while part of her was eager to continue, to discover what he was leading to. The atmosphere in the tiny dressing room had become too intimate and she was afraid. Afraid that she might reveal herself and her feelings, afraid that Worthing was about to say something she wasn't sure she wanted to hear.

She jumped as he reached over to place his hand on hers. "Stone," he said, his voice soft. "Stone, I—what *is* your first name?"

She was too startled to invent something. "Christabel," she said with a nervous laugh.

"Christabel," he repeated, "you know that I like you very much."

"I like you, too, Mr. Worthing," she said matter-of-factly, and tried to remove her hand from his, but he tightened his grasp.

"I feel that you are my friend," he continued. "We have worked together closely this last month or so and I have come to know you almost as well as I know myself."

She finally tore her hand away and stood up, moving a few paces away from him. "I fear you do not know me at all, Mr. Worthing, and would be most grievously disappointed to discover the truth about me."

He laughed at this and stood up, taking both her hands in his. "You sound as though you are harboring some deep, dark secret."

"I am," she said simply.

"Indeed?" He continued to smile with amusement. "It makes little difference to me, for I know *you* and I still maintain that I like you."

"But you do not love me?" She had to ask it.

"Do not complicate things," he said, dropping her hands. "I have told you before that I do not know what love means. Explain it to me—perhaps by your definition I do."

"If you did, you would know, you would not need me to explain."

"I suppose you are right." He had a sudden, fleeting memory of the kisses he had exchanged with Lady Jane Seymour at the ball. He had successfully put it out of his mind, and the remembrance of it now, in this context, disturbed him, even as he felt the pleasant tingle that always accompanied the memory. But he shook himself out of it, remembering his earlier words about liking and loving, and also remembering the decision he had come to two days ago. Now was the perfect time to act on that decision.

"Christabel," he said, still hesitant.

"Yes?"

He tried to form the words in his mind, but just as he was about to speak them, he was interrupted by a stern voice in the hallway.

"I am looking for Mr. Santanos." It was the duke of Duxton.

"He's in the theater setting up," came the reply.

"Kindly inform him that the duke of Duxton wishes to speak with him."

"Indeed, yer grace? I'm thinking he can't be disturbed now and you'll just have to wait yer turn." The voice was cocky. "So if you was to go along that corridor to the theater you could wait there until he had a moment free. Yer Grace."

The duke made a sound of impatience. "But there is no performance tonight, why should he be busy?"

"To be sure there is, Yer Grace. A special performance by the gentry. You might be wishful of staying to watch it."

"No, thank you. Be so good as to tell Santanos that I will wait for him in Miss Nichols's dressing room."

"I can't let you do that, Yer Grace. Not without leave from Miss Nichols. How am I to know you won't be walking off with some valuables, and me left to take the blame?"

"My good man, surely you have seen me here often enough. I assure you, I have no wish to steal anything. I simply want a quiet place to meet with Santanos."

From the first sound of the duke's voice Christabel and Worthing were alert, listening eagerly for anything he might say that they could use as evidence against him. But when he mentioned that he wished to enter the room, they looked at each other with horror, and now, as the argument outside continued, an argument in hushed tones was waged within as well.

"We can hide in here," Christabel said, picking up the candle and moving toward the door to the costume room.

188

"I will not go lurking in cupboards," Worthing said obstinately.

"It is not a cupboard, it is another room, and there is an exit from it into the hallway." She had moved toward the door by now and opened it, shining the candle in to show him that it was, indeed, a good-sized room, even while it was filled by boxes and racks of clothing. "Hurry, he'll be coming in here any minute. You don't wish to be discovered, do you?"

"Why not?" Worthing asked, his jaw jutting stubbornly. "It may be the best solution to confront him here and now."

"Don't be a fool!" Christabel hissed. "It would be much better to hide in here and hear what he has to say to Santanos."

But still Worthing wavered. Christabel's reasoning made sense, but he had spent too much of his life tackling problems head-on and still thought that was the best solution, even in this. The voices outside became louder as the duke had evidently convinced the other that he should be allowed admittance. Christabel pulled on Worthing's arm, but he continued to resist, and finally she gave up, deciding that if he wished to risk discovery, that was his affair, but it was better for her to remain concealed so they might retain some advantage over the duke. She shut the door behind her just as the outer door opened.

The duke entered with Freddie behind him, carrying a lamp, but when he saw Worthing he stopped short just inside the doorway, stunned.

"Worthing! What on earth are you doing here?"

"This is a right popular meeting place," Freddie said, putting the lamp down on the table and proceeding to light some of the other fixtures in the room. "Come to rob us all blind, I'll be bound. Now you chaps just wait here quietlike while I go fetch the hauthorities."

"That won't be necessary," the duke said, taking command of the situation. "I will vouch for this man."

"That's all very well, but 'ow am I to know you ain't in this together?" Freddie protested.

"Leave!" the duke boomed, and the look in his eye was so fearful Freddie immediately backed out.

"All right, then, but I'll be out 'ere in the 'allway if you try to make off with anything."

The duke closed the door behind him and turned back to Worthing. "Well, Worthing, you have not answered my question, What are you doing here, skulking about in the dark?"

Although he had been momentarily discomfited when the duke first entered, Worthing had by now recovered himself and countered him easily, "I might well ask the same of you, Duxton."

"Nonsense! I have an excellent reason for being here." He avoided Worthing's gaze. "I had an appointment with Miss Nichols."

"Indeed? That is very interesting, considering how adamant you were in your demands to see Santanos just a few minutes ago." As the duke blustered, Worthing relaxed to lean against the door to the costume room. "And Miss Nichols is not here, as you can see. She does not even have a performance tonight. You will have to give me a better answer than that, Duxton."

The duke laughed nervously. "What is the matter with you, Worthing? What difference does it make to you what appointments I have?"

"Perhaps a great deal of difference, when they are with men such as Santanos."

The duke attempted to regain the advantage. "At least I do not keep my appointments in darkened rooms, Worthing. Just what are you up to here?"

But Worthing was not be be bullied now. "Let us say a matter of business—perhaps the same business that brought you here."

The duke's eyes narrowed. "And what would you know of my business here?"

Worthing shrugged. "Perhaps nothing, perhaps a great deal. I may only say that after our conversation the other day about theaters I find it very curious to discover you are a frequent visitor here."

"Yes, I found that conversation curious, too, but it is even more curious that you have not yet given me a good explanation for your presence here now."

"Nor have you," Worthing countered. He seemed to be getting nowhere with the duke, but was reluctant to be the first to bring up the matter of the lost ships and Santanos's possible connection with them. It would be much better if he allowed the duke to mention this first, thus giving himself away. But the duke was being too cagey for that.

"See here, Worthing, this is beginning to look mighty suspicious to me. I walk into Miss Nichols's dressing room to find you lurking in the dark, avoiding every direct question I put to you."

"Let us say, then, that I am here to see the

revue by our respected friends and colleagues. I had hoped to find it a most illuminating performance."

The duke's eyes narrowed again. "Did you, by God? I never knew you to be enchanted with mediocrity."

"Nor am I, but I am interested in the agent of it, this certain Santanos whom you have the appointment with. And who, I might mention, has been seen in Southampton and Dover at very interesting times."

"So that's it, is it!" the duke exclaimed. "Well, you have been very clever about it, Worthing, but you won't get away with it!"

"And how will you prevent me from taking action, Duxton?" Worthing asked him, confident now that he had just heard what seemed to be the duke's admission of guilt. "How will you prevent me from—"

"This is how," the duke said, reaching into his pocket and pulling out something that gleamed in the lamplight.

Every muscle in Worthing's body tightened as he saw what the duke was holding. While small, the pistol was doubtless deadly, and it was pointed straight at his heart. "I didn't know you carried a pistol for your appointments, but I suppose I should have guessed."

"I have carried it since my unfortunate encounter with footpads last week, but I did not realize I would be forced to use it against someone I thought was a friend."

Worthing reached behind him, searching for the doorknob. He wished now that he had put more faith in Christabel's assertions of the duke's guilt but until five minutes ago he still did not quite believe them, and even one minute ago he would not have believed Duxton to be dangerous.

"Now we are going to start all over again," Duxton said, taking a step toward him. "Beginning with an explanation for your presence here tonight."

Worthing still could not reach the doorknob, but as he leaned against the door it suddenly opened behind him, and he stumbled into the arms of the woman waiting on the other side.

"Ooo, lovey, if I'd known you was all that eager I would 'ave 'urried," she exclaimed in a piercing Cockney voice. Worthing managed to stop himself from falling by grasping her trim waist, and looked up with astonishment at the beautiful face, somewhat marred by two intense spots of rouge.

"And who's yer friend 'ere?" she asked, squinting at the duke. "Lor' lumme! 'E's got a popper!"

Chapter Fourteen

The duke was no less astonished than Worthing a
the sight of this apparition and lowered his gun.

"Who are you?" he asked finally, as she helped
Worthing to his feet.

"I'm Molly Devlin, if you must know," she replied
insolently, "and now you tell me why you're waving
that popper around at my gentleman friend 'ere." She
did not wait for a reply but turned to Worthing and
continued, her voice somewhat softened, " 'As 'e 'urt
you, Justin? My poor baby, 'as 'e done you any 'arm?"

Worthing suddenly laughed. "No, thanks to you,
Molly, my dear." And he took her once more by the
waist and gave her a great, smacking kiss on the lips.

Molly's blush was barely discernible beneath the
two vivid spots of rouge as she said, "Oo, you are
'andful, you are."

The duke, who had been watching this performance with some embarrassment, finally pieced
things together in his mind and, returning the pistol

o his pocket, said, "Look here, Worthing, if you were meeting someone here, why didn't you just say so?"

"Perhaps I did not wish to compromise Miss Devlin," he said, and Molly giggled at the absurdity of this. "But while my presence here is now explained, yours is still not."

"Never mind about that, Justin," Molly said, disentangling herself from his grasp and moving toward the duke, flashing her green eyes provocatively. "Now, that 'e's 'ere, why shouldn't 'e join in the fun, too? What's yer name then, luv?" She sidled up to him, squeezing his arm.

"I have a previous engagement," he said stiffly.

She slipped her arm around his ample waist. "Sure you do, with us. Come on—'ave a bit of fun. There's always plenty to drink at these dos and we can find a nice little armful for you, can't we, Justin?" She gave Worthing a broad wink as she chucked the duke under the chin.

Worthing could barely contain his laughter at this sight, but he managed to say, "Well, Duxton, will you join us?"

"Duxton!" Molly shrieked unexpectedly. "Not the *duke* of Duxton? Well, fancy that! I'm yer long-lost niece what you must 'ave 'eard of!" She turned to Worthing. "Imagine that, Justin, 'ere's my long-lost uncle, the duke. Do you know me, uncle? Ain't I like me mother?"

The duke, wholly against his will, looked at her more closely and did indeed see the resemblance, much to his dismay.

"Oh, uncle!" Molly cried, throwing her arms round his neck and shouting so shrilly he flinched. "You simply *must* stay and party with us tonight. I want to 'ear all about me mother. Look, 'ere's Freddie now—'e'll show you where to go."

Freddie, hearing the commotion, had opened the door to see what was going on and was nearly as surprised as the other two men had been at the sight of Christabel in yet another disguise. "Miss Devlin! What—"

"'Ere, Freddie. Show the duke where to go and we'll be along presently." The duke hardly would have needed a guide, for the sounds of revelry could already be heard from the theater as the audience assembled for the entertainment of seeing the aristocracy perform their own works. But Freddie took his arm firmly and led him out the door, saying "This way, Yer Grace."

As soon as they had left, she turned to Worthing and handed him the duke's gun.

He took it with astonishment. "How did you—?" he asked with a wondering glance, meaning not only the gun but also her appearance there.

"We *may* be able to make something of this yet if you don't botch it up again," Christabel said sharply in her natural voice.

"But Miss Devlin, I don't quite understand. Are you a friend of Stone's? Where has she gone?"

Christabel looked at him with exasperation. "Oh, you *are* dense!" she exclaimed. "I am Stone."

This piece of information was almost too much for Worthing. Not only had he suddenly found again his elusive Lady Jane, but he was now told that he had had her all along in the unlikely person of Miss Stone.

"Do come," she said, taking his arm firmly, "and try to keep your eyes open, for I can't help you there. I can barely see a thing without my spectacles."

He stopped, pulling his arm in so that she wa

carried with it. He looked down into the pair of green eyes that had been haunting his dreams for days, try as he might to banish them. "Is the duke really your uncle?" he asked.

"Yes, but what difference does that make?"

"None," Worthing answered, smiling, "none whatsoever, as far as I am concerned." He was about to kiss her again, but she broke away impatiently.

"Come on. If we don't go in now, we may miss the entire purpose of our visit here tonight."

He did not argue, but followed her obediently through the hallway, which after several turns brought them to the side door of the auditorium.

The spectacle therein was one he had often heard of but never seen. He was surprised to recognize a number of his friends, who never would have set foot here otherwise, making themselves comfortable in the footmen's seats, some with blousy women on their knees. The stage itself was a blaze of lights and a hum of activity, and Worthing recognized Lord Ingram Westham directing the placement of several flats, painted to look like a street in Rome. He noticed, too, several veiled women entering a box up above, and smiled to himself. So there *was* a way for ladies to view the proceedings, although they did not care to set foot down below. He recalled hearing of the masquerades that were occasionally given in theaters, which afforded them a different kind of opportunity for mingling with the others undetected. Tonight that would be impossible, except, it seemed, for the surprising Miss Devlin.

Christabel led him to a seat on the aisle and promptly plopped herself on his lap. But the slight squeeze he gave her was met by a glare and a warning.

"Try that again and I'll pinch you black and blue," she said under her breath. "I will do all the necessary acting." Then she giggled shrilly and leaned closer to him, one arm around his neck.

"Do you see a small, swarthy man?" she asked. He nodded. "That is Santanos—keep an eye on him, note whom he speaks to."

Just then a familiar face came up and exclaimed, "Worthing! Never thought to see you here! And I see you've a sweet little armful, too." He gave Christabel a playful pinch on the cheek.

She giggled and said to Worthing in her shrill Cockney, "Ooo—who's yer good-looking friend, Justin?"

"Molly, this is Percy Waters."

"Hello, pretty Molly," he said, ruffling her hair. Worthing felt a glimmer of annoyance, not that Percy had done so, but that Christabel had not prevented him.

"Pretty Molly," Percy repeated, raising his glass to her and sloshing some wine in the process. "If I didn't have my piece all ready for tonight, I would write one especially for your green eyes. 'Two Twinkling Emerald Lights,' or something like that." He bowed and staggered slightly, for despite the fact that his wine kept sloshing out of his glass, he had obviously managed to get quite a bit inside him already. "But I notice you have nothing to drink, Worthing. Shall I fetch something for you and your sweet Molly?"

"No, thank you, Percy m'dear," Christabel said and giggled, "Justin 'ere is better without, if yo' know what I mean." She gave him a broad wink.

Percy laughed loudly at this, and with a nudge

198

nd a wink at Worthing left them to greet another of
is friends who had just arrived.

With a great effort Worthing heaved Christabel
ff his lap and onto the bench beside him. "What
id you mean by that remark?" he asked angrily.

"Hush, I suspect the duke is watching us. You
night at least try to give a convincing performance."

"I thought you were going to do all the acting."

"Yes, as well as everything else. I suppose when
he time comes I will be the one to hold both the
uke and Santanos at gunpoint while you flounder
round in a quandary of indecision." She glared at
im, then a moment later they both laughed.

"This is no time to lose our tempers," Worthing
aid.

"No, you are right. We must be alert and try not to
rouse the duke's suspicions even more than you
ave already." Then she put herself back on his lap,
ne arm cozily encircling his shoulder.

Duxton was indeed watching them, but was so far
om having his suspicions aroused that he had
early forgotten his own purpose there that night.
'o say he was shocked by Worthing's behavior
ould be an understatement, but it was not the mere
ight of one of his colleagues making free with an
ctress in public that he found shocking, for wher-
ver he cared to look in the theater a similar sight
reeted his eyes. No, it was the fact that the actress
Vorthing was carrying on with was the duke's own
iece. His meeting with her had confirmed his very
orst fears—to think that the daughter of his own
weet sister (suddenly he forgot all that he had
ormerly found reprehensible in her character)
nould have ended up no better than a common
oxy, vulgar of speech and excessive in dress. On top

of that was a certain disappointment in Alexis Nich
ols, who so frequently took pains to introduce he
stepdaughter into the conversation, praising he
gentle breeding and fine education. The truth was
sad blow to the duke, and he was so lost in his miser
that he missed the dubious pleasure of seeing S
Ashton Phelps perform a comic scene of his ow
devising with an actress of very ample proportior
and assorted props of a feather bed, a bottle
poison and a stuffed cat. He was not brought bac
to himself or his business at the theater until Sar
tanos, spotting him in the audience, came up t
speak to him.

Worthing noticed this immediately and pointed
out to Christabel. She removed herself from his la
so that he could wander, seemingly aimlessly, clos
enough to overhear their conversation. But just as h
was within earshot, the duke and Santanos move
into the hallway from a side door where they coul
converse without the distraction of Theodore Hoc
singing a bawdy song of his own composition to th
indifferent accompaniment of a brightly painte
young woman.

Worthing positioned himself so that he coul
watch them through the doorway, but he was onl
able to hear snippets of conversation, somethir
about "by the twentieth of June," and "the oth
principals were not yet decided upon." His heart wa
pounding as he fingered the pistol in his pocket. Th
noise in the theater had become much louder as th
audience was encouraged to join in on the verses
the song, but Worthing could hear enough to piece th
whole treacherous plot together. The duke wa
evidently discussing the arrangements Santanos ha
made in what must be a very complex spy networ

nd Worthing gasped when he caught a remark made
bout arms supplies for a company of soldiers. Did
heir plans also include an attack by enemy soldiers
n the very shores of England? He burned with new
ury at the perfidy of one who had been his mentor and
new now that when the moment for action arrived he
vould not be found wanting.

This moment came when he saw the duke remove
is pocketbook and begin counting out notes for
antanos. With a grand gesture made all the more
wful by the sudden silence in the house as a new act
as about to begin, he stepped into the hallway,
randishing the pistol.

"I have seen quite enough, Duxton," he said even-
y. "You will both come with me where I will turn you
ver to those who know how to deal with traitors
gainst the Crown. If you do not care to oblige me, I
m quite prepared to use this pistol."

The duke stared at him for a long moment, then
pluttered, "Have you gone mad, Worthing?"

"There is no need for further pretense, Duxton.
our little game has ended—I know *all.*"

"Game? What game? I really do believe you *have*
one mad."

"If you choose to cooperate, I will make it easy on
ou, Duxton. I'll see to it that you leave the country
ith a minimum of scandal. For of course your
ehavior reflects on the entire ministry and could
rove demoralizing were our troops to hear of it, with
our own son among them."

"Leave the country!" Duxton exclaimed. "You are
aving, Worthing! There's been something odd
bout your behavior all evening. I knew I should
ave followed my instincts earlier when I had the
hance."

"I am only glad that I finally followed mine," Worthing said. "Now come with me, please, you both have a great deal of explaining to do."

"Señor seems to be under a misapprehension," Santanos put in. "If I may speak for the most noble duke, Señor, may I say that he is so generously providing money so that our production of *Antony and Cleopatra* may be the most glorious in theatrical history. I know not what you are saying about traitors and scandal."

"A very nice, pat explanation," Worthing said. " wish that I could believe it."

"But it is true!" the duke exclaimed, very red i the face. "What did you think I was giving him th money for?"

The duke's earnestness and quite genuine in dignation began to tell on Worthing and once agai he entertained those doubts that had been plaguin him all along concerning Duxton's guilt. But th pistol in his hand did not waver. "Then do you den you have been selling our secrets to the French?"

"What?" The duke was livid. "Is that what yo think of me? But you are the one who was—"

"Señors, please," Santanos interrupted. "You argument is beginning to disturb my most nobl patrons. I beg of you to be quiet and Señor—if yo could put your gun away?" he asked this graciousl "Might I also point out, Señor Duke, that your son i about to begin his piece and I always find him mos entertaining. Perhaps you would care to hear hin too." Ignoring Worthing's still pointed gun, h walked casually back into the theater.

Worthing glanced at the pistol as though it ha become an unnecessary appendage that should b lopped off, and replaced it in his pocket with som

202

embarrassment. "Look here, Duxton, you still have some explaining to do. If your purposes here are as innocent as you say, then why did you not tell me earlier?"

"*You* were the one I found lurking in a darkened room! I am quite convinced you have gone mad."

Worthing protested and they continued the argument heatedly, but in lowered tones, and as a result missed much of Lord Ingram's quite acceptable performance.

Christabel, meanwhile, had remained in her seat, trusting Worthing to take care of the duke at this point, for she no longer cared. It had suddenly hit her that her disguise as Miss Stone was ruined and she might never again enjoy the easy companionship with Worthing that she had come to value above all else. And what was it he had been about to say to her before they had been interrupted in Alexis's dressing room? She was certain at that time that he was actually going to propose to her, and while she had thought then that she did not want him to continue, for his proposal would not have been accompanied by any words of love, she realized now that that was exactly what she had always hoped for. For Worthing had thought he was proposing to plain, unattractive Miss Stone, not the beautiful Christabel Devlin, and what was more he had told her in so many words that he *liked* her. Was that not what she had been seeking all her adult life? Someone who liked her for herself, or what she was inside, and not someone who had merely fallen in love with her appearance.

But now things could never be the same again. Doubtless Worthing's liking would cease now that he knew what a trick she had played on him, and without Worthing her future was bleak. There was some consolation in the knowledge that with the duke out of the way she might yet be accepted by her family, for had not Lord Ingram promised his friendship? But this was small recompense now for all she had lost.

So deep in thought was she that she did not even notice the approach of Percy Waters, who had seen she was left alone, nor did she hear him address her nor note his subsequent withdrawal as he decided she must be in a drunken stupor and therefore not much use to him. She finally came to herself again when she heard Lord Ingram announced as the next performer. He now seemed to be the only hope for her future, so she gave him her attention, which was rewarded by hearing him recite, in a quite melodious voice, a comic poem touching on the indiscretions of the Prince of Wales. This attention only wandered when she noticed some movement by the side door and saw indistinctly a shape that seemed to be Santanos reenter the theater. She wondered what Worthing could be about to let him slip away like that and moved closer to the Spaniard so she could see him more clearly.

Lord Ingram began his second poem, which was something in the pastoral tradition and lent itself even better than his first piece to his elocutionary skills. Oddly, as he had begun, Santanos had removed a memorandum book from his pocket and was taking notes, and as Lord Ingram began the second stanza, Christabel noted with a start that there was something terribly familiar about the pattern of his verse. The poem itself made little sense, but seemed to be composed entirely for the purpose of listing flowering species of plants, some of them repeated, and some spoken of in numbers, as in the line "a thousand twenty amaryllis decked her gown."

Christabel moved swiftly to the doorway to discover what had become of Worthing. She found him still engaged in an argument with the duke, which by now was peppered with strong language and stronger mutual accusations. Without wasting a second, she poked Worthing sharply in the ribs and said in a harsh whisper,

"You fools! While you stand here bickering, Lord Ingram is describing in minute detail to Santanos the route of the *Venture* and the stores she is carrying down to the last bullet!"

The next few minutes were total confusion. In an instant both Worthing and the duke knew exactly what was happening, and in that same instant they both acted, Worthing heading for Santanos and the duke for his son. Both barreled into Percy Waters, who had followed "Pretty Molly" to the back of the theater, and in the next instant the three men were nothing but a tangle of legs and arms. Others there, most of them quite as drunk as Percy, thought it was a row and eagerly ran over to join in whichever side seemed to need them, and in less than ten seconds it turned into a free-for-all, with some of the women throwing oranges into the melee and everyone punching anyone they were sober enough to see straight.

Christabel, squinting hard, saw Santanos making for the door. Worthing saw him too, and started pursuit, pulling the pistol out of his pocket as he ran. The duke, meanwhile, had managed to extricate himself from Percy Waters and made his way to the stage, jumping up with an agility he had not known since he was a boy. Lord Ingram, unaware of the cause of the fight, stood gaping and annoyed that his recital had been interrupted. He did not notice his father until too late, and the duke, taking his example from those below him, punched his son in the eye.

A few minutes later, they were back in Alexis's dressing room, Christabel bathing Lord Ingram's face and the duke in a towering rage.

"To think that a son of mine should sink so low! Did you not once think of the lives at stake? The hundred or so men who have become prisoners of the French because of your actions? Your own brother desperately in need of the supplies you so casually donated to our worst enemy! If I did not know better I would say your mother had played me false, for you are no son of mine! I only thank God she is not with us to see this iniquity! Why did you do it, Ingram, why?"

"For the money," Lord Ingram said, so flippantly that Christabel was tempted to let his head drop and indeed did press so hard with the cloth that he winced.

"Yes, Ingram always did tell me that he would do a great deal for money," said a new voice at the door. It was Lady Imogen, who had been the veiled figure in the box seat.

"And did you know about this, too?" the duke demanded, turning on her.

"No, Father, I did not," she said calmly, "but I must admit I wondered why Ingram had not been complaining of lack of money lately. I thought you had raised his allowance."

The duke groaned and clutched his aching side, which he had strained by his leap onto the stage. Christabel left Lord Ingram's side and went to help her uncle into a chair. "You will burst a blood vessel if you continue in this way," she chided him.

"Well, if it isn't the elusive Miss Devlin," Lady Imogen said, noticing her with some surprise.

"Greetings, coz," Christabel answered with an ironic smile.

"You are much what I expected," Lady Imogen said. She took a seat beside her brother and said languidly, "You are a greater fool than even I thought you could be, Ingram."

Christabel excused herself momentarily as she went into the costume room to find her spectacles; she was tired of seeing everything in a blur. She wiped some of the paint off her face, too, before she came back into the room where her uncle had once again leapt to his feet to rant.

"Uncle," she said gently, "do sit down and compose yourself." She reached into the cupboard where Alexis kept the decanter of sherry and offered the duke a glass. He took it gratefully and sat down, drinking it all in one gulp. As he handed the glass back to Christabel, he saw her again as if for the first time. "You—you're quite different," he said in some confusion.

"I put my spectacles on," she explained.

"Yes, of course, your—your dear mother was short-sighted, too. You're very like her."

"So I have been told," Christabel said, and the expression on the duke's face was so woebegone and desolate that quite unexpectedly her heart went out to him and she felt ashamed of her previous attitude toward him. She refilled his glass and handed it back to him tenderly.

"Look here," Lady Imogen said sharply, "this family reunion is very touching, but what is to be done

207

now? Father, I won't stand for a scandal. It will ruin me forever and ruin all my chances with Worthing."

Christabel gave an involuntary "Humph."

"And as for you—*cousin*," Lady Imogen continued, turning on her. "I would like very much to know what your part is in all of this. Don't think I didn't notice how you were carrying on with Worthing in the theater. Are you his mistress? Because if you are, I will have a thing or two to say about *that!*"

Christabel flushed and was about to retort, but the duke spoke first, "That is not the kind of language I expect to hear from my daughter," he said sternly. "We have much to thank your cousin for, Imogen. It was she who discovered this treachery of your brother's and thereby exposed a most insidious plot."

"And thereby expose our whole family to the most horrible scandal. If I am cut in society, I shall have little to thank my cousin for, Father."

"There will be no scandal. Ingram will leave the country as quietly as possible and I hope never to hear from him again."

Ingram, nursing his eye, had paid little attention to the conversation until now, and with this he sat up indignantly, "So that's what you plan for me?"

A further tirade from the duke was halted when Christabel exclaimed, "Thank God!" She had gone to stand in the doorway, for she had become worried by Worthing's prolonged absence and began to imagine him lying in a gutter with his head bashed in. But now he came in, dirty and disheveled perhaps but his head intact. Christabel poured him a glass of sherry while he caught his breath.

"What a stroke of luck!" he exclaimed. "I chased

him for two blocks, but I never would have caught him if he hadn't run smack into Lord Liverpool himself leaving a performance at the Drury Lane. He's taking him in now, so I came back here to let you know. Lady Imogen, I didn't see you, what are you doing here? I'll have another glass of this, Christabel, if you don't mind. And as for you—" He raised his arm as if ready to make Lord Ingram's eyes a matched pair, but Christabel held him back, saying,

"Justin! We've had quite enough fisticuffs for the evening." She turned to pour him another glass of sherry and another for the duke.

Lady Imogen was at once charming and attentive. "Do take my seat, Justin, you look quite done in." She took the glass of sherry from Christabel and offered it solicitously to him.

"Thank you, Lady Imogen," he said. "So what do you think of Miss Devlin now? I say she deserves a decoration from the Crown at the very least. It was on her account alone that we traced the thing this far, although I must admit, Duxton, it was on her account, too, that I thought you were the culprit, but she straightened us all out in the end. Lady Imogen, why didn't you tell me Miss Devlin was your cousin when I asked after her the other day?"

"I prefer not to acknowledge it," Lady Imogen said coldly.

"Oh, good," Christabel said, as though she was relieved. "I prefer not to acknowledge you, either." Lady Imogen was most put out to hear Worthing laugh at this.

The duke raised his head and finally spoke again. "Ingram, you will leave the country on the next ship. I will give you money for your passage and some to go on, but if you ever set foot in England again, I will see to it personally that you hang by the neck until you are dead."

Lord Ingram, who was engaged in writing a note shrugged his shoulders indifferently at this pronouncement and there was a short, uncomfortable silence in the room.

Worthing broke it. "Look here, Duxton, there is something I still can't understand. If you had nothing to do with this matter, then why were you giving Santanos money for a company of soldiers?"

"A company of soldiers?" the duke repeated with a puzzled expression. Then he managed a short laugh. "We were discussing the properties needed for the soldiers in *Antony and Cleopatra*. He wanted rather more than he told me at first."

Worthing shook his head. "And why the deuce didn't you tell me you were financing a production when we were in this room before? It would have saved a good deal of misunderstanding."

"I—uh—"

"I think the duke was hesitant to admit to his generosity," Christabel put in. "He has something of a reputation to uphold."

"Yes, and look where that has led me," the duke said miserably. "My own son—" He gave a little moan and buried his head in his hands once more.

Lord Ingram handed a folded note to his sister. "Well, why are we all sitting about here? If I am to leave the country, I hope you will at least let me go home to pack."

"Yes, and you might pack this along with everything else, for I don't want it any longer," Christabel said, and she reached in her pocket to hand him the pearl stickpin.

210

Ingram took it with bewilderment. "I don't understand? How did you get this? I gave it to—" He looked at her more closely and suddenly laughed. "I see we have a better actor than I in the family."

"Ingram, your amusement is singularly ill-placed in this situation," the duke said sternly, taking him by the arm. "Come along now. Miss Devlin—Christabel, may I see you home? I assume you are residing with your stepmother."

"No, indeed," Worthing said. "She lives with me."

"What!" The new tenderness that had been in the duke's eyes for his niece left him abruptly. "Then what Imogen said is true!"

"I don't know what Lady Imogen said, and I don't know why you should be surprised by Christabel's place of residence. You have seen her there yourself on at least one occasion that I know of."

The duke continued to regard him coldly, joined by the equally cold glare of his daughter.

"Really, Justin," Lady Imogen said, "you might at least spare me this humiliation. To actually *flaunt* your mistress before me—"

"Lady Imogen, if you please!" Worthing interrupted. "Miss Stone is not now, nor ever will be, my *mistress.*"

"Stone!" Lady Imogen cried.

"Of course!" the duke exclaimed. "I see it now. Why didn't you tell me, girl?"

"If you will excuse me," Lady Imogen said proudly, "my maid has been awaiting me in the hallway." Then with a last look at Christabel and an almost imperceptible sniff, she left the room, saying, "I always knew there was something *peculiar* about you."

Chapter Fifteen

"She is too! She is too!" Richard, the fifth earl o
Fenworth was crying in very unearl-like tones, em
phasizing each word by slamming his tiny fist on th
table.

"Don't be a silly little boy," Miss Jones saic
severely.

"I am not a little boy!" Richard shouted. "I'm
handsome prince in disguise and Stoney is a beau
tiful princess under a 'chantment."

"Miss Stone is your uncle's secretary," Miss Jone
said firmly, with a slight note of disapproval as sh
described her predecessor's position. "She is not
princess in disguise and you are a naughty little boy
not a prince."

"She is too! She is too! She is too!" Richar
persisted, jumping up and running to the door. "I'
prove it to you—just come and ask her. She'll te
you that it's true!"

Miss Jones started after him, thinking that h

eally *was* a naughty little boy and how very tired
he was of chasing after him. "Richard, you come
back here this instant! We must get on with your
lessons." This was ended with a futile little sigh, for
he knew that Richard's lessons would not begin
again until he had his way. Really, a most stubborn
and willful child and she must speak to her employer
about him.

Richard had run down the hallway and was pounding on Christabel's door, shouting, "Stoney, you
how her." Miss Jones trotted behind him.

When Christabel opened the door Richard was
not at all surprised to see her without her disfiguring
paint, in a close fitting dress that showed off her
figure, her hair arranged attractively in ringlets
round her face.

"There!" he exclaimed triumphantly. "What did
tell you?"

Miss Jones, on the other hand, was flabbergasted
and stood there gaping, her hand fluttering to her
breast to still the rapid beating of her heart. Really,
he *must* speak to her employer, this post was not
agreeing with her at all.

Richard then noticed the case that Christabel
carried and that the room behind her had been
stripped of all her personal effects.

"You're not leaving?" he asked with dismay.

"I'm afraid I must, Richard," Christabel said qui-
tly "As you can see, the enchantment has been
lfted from me and I am now free to go."

Even as he comprehended the magical logic of
his, Richard was not quite ready to accept her
departure calmly. "But you can't go! Who will pro-
ect me from the wicked sorcerer?"

Christabel smiled wryly at Miss Jones, who appeared to be about to faint. "Miss Jones will have to do her best, Richard." She bent down and kissed him on the forehead. "I will miss you, but you must be glad for me because I am no longer under a terrible spell."

Richard nodded miserably, bravely holding back his tears.

"Goodbye, Miss Jones," Christabel said pleasantly, extending her hand. Miss Jones took it briefly and timidly, then Christabel picked up her case and started down the back stairs.

As soon as she was out of sight Miss Jones exclaimed, "Well, I never!" and Richard broke into lusty sobs.

An hour later the duke of Duxton was announced to Justin Worthing, who was in his library bravely carrying on with the morning's work alone, for he thought Christabel was still abed and did not wish to disturb her after the night they had had.

"Ah, Duxton," he said pleasantly. "I suppose you have matters well in hand."

The duke looked tired and worn this morning; he had spent a sleepless night reflecting on the treachery of his son and how very much he might have done to prevent it if only he had been a bit more generous. But such musings were useless, as he discovered; the damage was done. The great thing now was to avoid a scandal, for no shadow of his brother's deed must ever fall upon his eldest son, the marquess of Westbridge, the heir to his coronet.

"I have booked passage for Ingram on a ship that sails this afternoon for the West Indies. I've offered him the stewardship of my estates there, he can take it or leave it, as he pleases. And he shan't think he

214

will receive them on my death, either, for I am changing my will. That's one thing I want to discuss with you, Worthing. This niece of mine, I must say I still can't believe she was your Miss Stone. She looked so different."

"I know," Worthing agreed ruefully. "I would like to speak to you about her, too. I think we both have an interest in her future."

He ordered refreshments as the two men sat down for an amiable chat about Miss Devlin, which fortunately had the happy effect of taking the duke's mind off his son for the moment. For, as he said, even though he had lost a son, he had at least gained some compensation in the form of a very resourceful and courageous niece. And, unbeknownst to Christabel herself, in the matter of a few minutes she had been transformed from a penniless orphan without prospects, to a young lady of quality with a vast and noble family, quite a tidy portion, and a most suitable future.

Their chat was interrupted some minutes later by the most frightfully heartrending sobs it had ever been their misfortune to hear.

"Good God, that sounds like Phoebe!" Worthing cried, jumping up. "Whatever can be the matter?"

"Ah, I hoped she would not take it so hard," the duke said, also leaping to his feet. "Imogen is up here with her and I fear she must have just broken the news about Ingram to her."

They both rushed up the stairs to see if they could offer any aid, only to find Lady Fenworth already surrounded by a number of people offering her water as Dorcas tried to bathe her temples with a damp cloth.

Richard stood beside her, saying things like, "Really, Mama, it is all for the best, don't you see?" and Miss Jones stood in the background looking disap proving. As soon as she noticed Worthing at th door, she determined to speak to him. Really, sh could not remain here any longer, it was too tryin on her delicate nerves.

"What's this all about?" the duke demanded i his booming voice.

Lady Imogen, who was also standing by feelin rather disgusted at Phoebe's outburst, answere him, "Really, Father, it's too bad. I told her all abou Ingram and gave her his note, and she read it, takin the whole quite calmly, I thought. Then she said sh must discuss it with Stone of all people, and whe she discovered that Stone had gone, she becam most frightfully upset."

Poor Phoebe was almost smothered by th number of servants offering her assistance, and th duke shouted for them to all leave her be as he wen to her himself.

"My dear lady, calm yourself, please," he said taking her hand tenderly.

She looked up at him with her large trustin brown eyes and was somewhat soothed. "Oh, is it a true?"

The duke stroked her hair gently, much to th amazement of his daughter, and said, "I'm afraid s my dear, but you must find the strength to deal wit it." Over her shoulder he gave the rest of the com pany such a fierce glance that they could have n doubt of his wish to be alone with Lady Fenworth fc the moment, and so they cleared out, Dorcas seem ing to be the only one who had a look of suprem contentment upon her face.

Left alone with the duke, Phoebe ceased her tear

as she thought vaguely what a nice, *comforting* man he was, and how very like her dear papa whom she had missed for many years. She was further comforted when he discovered that her anguish was not because of the imminent departure of Lord Ingram nor even the fact that he had written her a note asking her to join him, but the terrible departure of Stone; for then he was able to assure her that she would see as much of Stone as ever she could wish, for Stone was actually his niece and he hoped he could remain on terms of affection with both ladies. This was entirely satisfactory to Phoebe, as was the kiss the duke gave her, and she reflected that it was very lucky that Ingram was no longer around, for she had never really understood him, but the duke spoke so *clearly* and so *understandably* that she never seemed to be at a loss with him.

Meanwhile, in the hallway, Lady Imogen, Miss Jones and Richard were all trying to speak to Worthing at once.

"—and her 'chantment wored off, so I suppose she went back to her palace—"

"—and the strain on my nerves is too great—"

"—and the silly creature took on so I didn't know what to do—"

It was Richard he grasped on as being most likely to tell him what he really wanted to know—whether Stone had indeed left the house.

"Oh, yes, and she was ever so beautiful, too," Richard told him readily. "And she said the 'chantment was over and I wasn't to take on too much."

"Really, Mr. Worthing, the boy is quite incorrigible. How am I to teach him his declensions when all he will speak of is enchantments and magic?"

"Miss Jones, I will speak to you later. Take Rich-

217

ard upstairs for now, I am getting the deuce of a headache."

With this Lady Imogen became all sympathy and consolation. "I don't wonder at it with all that has been happening since last night," she murmured, leading him downstairs to the morning room. "I have been up most the night helping Ingram to pack, but I must admit he has no sympathy from me." Worthing sat down wordless, only half listening to her ramblings, and she rang the bell to order some refreshment for him.

"Have you anything cold to drink?" she asked Saunders when he came in. "I think a glass of lemonade would be just the thing."

"Certainly, your ladyship," he said, and bowed out. He returned shortly with the drink, and meanwhile Lady Imogen had continued to murmur soothing words to Worthing, showing him how very sympathetic and kind she could be.

"Thank you, Lady Imogen," he said at last, after drinking the lemonade. "Do you suppose she has gone to her stepmother's house? I expect your father would know where that is."

"What does it matter?" Lady Imogen said with a light laugh. "She is gone now, and perhaps it is better that way. She never made any but the most ill-natured remarks to me."

Worthing looked at her wryly. "No, I suppose she didn't. She was never one to hide her opinions."

Lady Imogen took the glass from him. "Your work will probably go much better for you now that you can find yourself a proper secretary."

"Do you think so?"

"Why, of course. My cousin is not a proper any

hing—certainly not a proper lady, the way she was ll tarted up last night."

"Lady Imogen!"

She laughed. "I am so sorry, Justin, you are right. hat is not at all language you should expect to hear rom me. But I shall learn to mend my ways for you, you wish it."

"There is no need for you to do anything at all for ie, Lady Imogen," he said pleasantly. "Except, of ourse, all that might be expected from one cousin to nother, for that is what we shall be very soon, I ope." He ignored the sudden shock on her face and ook her by the shoulders, kissing her warmly on the heek. "Will that not be splendid? I know dear hoebe will be most pleased to hear that she is soon become related to you by marriage, for she thinks he world of you. But if you will excuse me now, Lady mogen, I wish to speak to your father. I am hoping e knows where Christabel might have gone."

He ran into the duke coming out of Lady enworth's chamber.

"Congratulate me, Worthing!" the duke cried adly, "I have been made the happiest of men."

Worthing was only gratified to see this pleasant hange in his friend's countenance, but he was con- used as to the origin of it. "What do you mean, uxton?"

"I mean that Lady Fenworth has consented to be y wife!"

Worthing was no less pleased to hear this than the uke was to announce it. "Why, that's splendid, uxton. And now, if you will be so kind as to tell me ne direction of Alexis Nichols, I hope that I will be ade equally as happy."

"And so you see, Alex, now there is really nothing else for me to do," Christabel was explaining, after telling her stepmother all about the events that had taken place the night before. "I absolutely *refuse* to seek another position as a governess, and the duke will certainly have nothing to do with me now he knows how I suspected him. Justin will not want to see me again after the trick I have played on him. The only thing left for me is to go on the stage—you can raise no objections now."

But Alexis was thinking something Christabel had told her earlier. "So he was financing a production for me, the silly man. And I'll wager he never would have told me, for he has a horror of being thought an easy touch."

Christabel slumped sullenly on the settee. "At least *your* future is assured. You will become the duke's mistress and be set up quite cozily."

Alexis laughed. "Of course I will not become his mistress, you silly child."

"Then why should he spend so much money on you?"

"For old time's sake, my dear. I knew the duke many years ago, when he was still the marquess of Westbridge. In face, he was the marquess who brought me here from Russia and helped me start in the theater."

Christabel sat up, astonished. "Why did you never tell me so?"

"My dear, I did not know that the marquess I knew so many years ago and the duke of Duxton were one and the same until I met him again for your sake. Then it did not seem like a good idea to tell you. You have been so against him and so ready to

220

elieve the worst of *me,* that I didn't think it wise to ll you."

"I am sorry, Alex," she said humbly, "I should ave had more faith in you."

"Indeed you should have. The duke and I met as ld friends and found we enjoyed each other's com-any. But so far from being his mistress, I have been e recipient of innumerable confidences about the oman he wishes to make his wife. Your little Lady enworth, as a matter of fact."

"He wishes to marry Phoebe?" Christabel ex-aimed, and then laughed. "It would be just the ing for her. I always thought Ingram was rather bove her head."

"Yes, he saw his son as the chief obstacle to his appiness, so I suppose there is now nothing to stand his way." She was thoughtful for a moment. "I onder if he could be persuaded to loan Martin the oney to buy the theater. Now that that little retch Santanos is taken care of, perhaps we might e able to build up a respectable company again. It ould take no more than he was willing to spend on roducing a show. I shall have to speak to him."

"And now we come back to the question of my ture," Christabel said, jumping up, "which you ave so carefully avoided during this whole con-rsation."

Alexis smiled mysteriously. "I have no doubts out your future, my dear."

"Then you will let me join the company?"

"Certainly not!"

Christabel gave a gasp of exasperation and was ut to launch once more into her reasons for want-g to come upon the stage, when the maid came in announce "Mr. Justin Worthing."

221

"There, you see," Alexis said, rising, "I told you had no doubts about your future."

Worthing was ushered in just as Alexis was abou to leave the room. "Mr. Worthing," she said pleas antly, "how nice to see you again. If you are in nee of a governess, I suggest you speak to my step daughter, but you will have to excuse me, for I hav a pressing engagement upstairs."

As soon as they were left alone, Worthing turne to Christabel. "And what are you doing here, any way?" he asked with a hint of annoyance. "Wh couldn't you stay put at my house?"

Christabel turned away from him and replie evenly, "I was sure you had no further use for m services as a secretary, so I left."

"And so I haven't!" he exclaimed.

"There, you see!"

"You know damn well that I want you to becom my wife."

She turned on him roundly. "I don't *damn we* know that, and if you are proposing to me, you migl at least do it civilly."

He was immediately contrite. "I am sorry, you a right as usual. Stone—Miss Devlin—Christabel— whatever you choose to call yourself, will you mar me?"

"No, thank you," she replied quietly.

"What do you mean—no? Must you give me argument about everything?"

"If you feel that way, then I don't see why you wis to marry me at all."

"You know how I feel about you. I felt sure, aft last night—and that you—" He stopped short, fru trated. It should have been so easy; he would as she would reply yes. But of course he should ha

222

nown that nothing could be so easy with the con-
ary Stone.

"Yes, I know that you *like* me," she said in a small
oice, "but are uncertain as to the matter of *love.*"

He breathed a sigh of relief—so that was all!
Must you remember everything I tell you?" He
ent up to her and took her by the shoulders. "I do
ve you—I know that now."

She was still not satisfied. "But whom do you love
e as? As Miss Stone? Or only as the beautiful Miss
evlin?"

"Why must you complicate everything?" He
ached down to kiss her, but she moved away.
here was a sudden droop to his shoulders. "Forgive
e, I have been very stupid. I suppose you do not
ve me."

"Oh, no, that's not it!" she cried before she had
me to think.

He smiled and took her back in his arms with a
rmer grip, allowing her no chance to escape. "Then
op this constant argument and tell me yes. Don't
u think we will have enough to argue about once
e are husband and wife?"

She looked up into his eyes and suddenly they
oth laughed together. "Yes, I suppose we will," she
id, and allowed him to kiss her this time, quite
tisfactorily.

If you have your heart set on Romance, read

Coventry Romances